MONSTER HUNTERS UNLIMITED

DEMONS AND ELEMENTALS

BY JOHN GATEHOUSE AND DAVE WINDETT

Pe

tiu
i
th
d
lur
f

PSS!
PRICE STERN SLOAN
An Imprint of Penguin Group (USA) LLC

For Cameron & for Charlotte, Elizabeth, and Ford—JG

To The P.S.F.G. You know who you are—DMW

PRICE STERN SLOAN
Published by the Penguin Group
Penguin Group (USA) LLC, 375 Hudson Street, New York, New York 10014, USA

USA | Canada | UK | Ireland | Australia | New Zealand | India | South Africa | China

penguin.com
A Penguin Random House Company

Library of Congress Cataloging-in-Publication Data is available.

ISBN 978-0-8431-6901-0   10 9 8 7 6 5 4 3 2 1

INTRODUCTION

The enemy is fear.

—Mahatma Gandhi (born Mohandas Karamchand Gandhi)

—India Civil Rights leader (1869–1948)

Ultra-cool dude Mahatma Gandhi (*Mahatma* means "great soul") knew what he was talking about: Show fear and you've had it!

This is why hard-core monster hunters never display such wimpy emotions during our gore-splattered battles with the hellish hordes of the underworld. (We may need the occasional pair of clean underwear, but fear? Nah!)

You bravehearts who have already signed up as members of the International Federation of Monster Hunters know what chills to expect from this book.

For the newbies among you: Welcome to something a million times worse than your very worst nightmares!

You are about to step over the threshold and into a world you never knew existed, one inhabited by terrors beyond your imagination!

Within these pages, you will discover the truth that governments the world over have tried for centuries to keep hidden from their citizens.

These regimes know that if the facts about what's "out there" become public knowledge, there will be mass hysteria and anarchy, chaos and insurrection. Our entire civilization will collapse, toppling once more back into the stygian abyss of nothingness.

Don't believe it? There have been successful civilizations before us, you know—some even more technologically advanced for their age than our own.

And we're not even talking about "lost" civilizations of which there is, at yet, little evidence that they actually existed. Like the one that apparently prospered on the giant continent of Lemuria (aka Mu) in the Indian Ocean, 78,000 years ago.

Or the great civilization that thrived on the island of Atlantis in the Atlantic Ocean and was first mentioned in the dialogues *Timaeus* and *Critias* written by ancient Greek philosopher and mathematician Plato (424/423 BC–348/347 BC).

Were they real? Fictional? We honestly don't know. No one does. But simply because there is currently no solid proof that something *was* doesn't mean that something wasn't. As professional monster hunters, our minds are open to all possibilities and conjectures!

However, there is ample evidence of ancient peoples who came before us and who kicked butt when it came to advanced technologies. They make our own pathetic achievements look puny by comparison.

Historians argue whether Mesopotamia (where modern-day Iraq resides) or ancient Egypt was the first of the great civilizations. Who cares? They were both around at least six thousand years ago, give or take a Saturday.

What matters is that the geniuses of Mesopotamia invented the wheel (you know, kind of important); writing (in cuneiform, a wedge-shaped writing on clay tablets); the first recognizable alphabet; many farm tools that are still in use today; metalworking; copper-working; textile-making; the concept of keeping time; the twelve-month calendar; mathematics; geometry; and possibly the first battery, to name but a few!

The Egyptians invented a type of paper called *papyrus* (although some say that the ancient Chinese invented paper as we know it in 160 BC); a written language style; black ink; the first (solar-based) calendar; the first (water-powered) clock; the sundial; surgical instruments; maps; mass production of pottery; the first ocean-crossing sailing boats; irrigation systems; a numbering system, including fractions; courts and a justice system; makeup; toothpaste; and breath mints.

While in the Mediterranean, the ancient Greeks invented the computer (a 2,000-year-old clockwork calculator was unearthed on the island of Antikythera in 1900—look it up if you don't believe us!); the first rudimentary steam engine (in 1 BC); automatic doors; vending machines; cranes; the musical keyboard; diving bells; the Olympics; democracy; the first alphabet with vowels; and the theater.

As for the ancient Romans, well, *fff*! Road-building; spinning and weaving; aqueducts; public baths; bridges; harbors and dams; concrete; street paving; glassblowing; glass windows; water mills; newspapers; books; policemen; firemen; central heating; indoor plumbing; flush toilets; language; and laws.

This is a mere handful of the many magnificent civilizations from times past. And where are they now? Collapsed into the dust of history, victims of the horrors and dread let loose by the infernal denizens from the fiery pits of purgatory and the dark dimensions!

Monster hunters are the frontline warriors in a never-ending war against the invading massed hordes of devils and demons, fiendish fae folk and vampires, werewolves and zombies, ghosts, man-monsters, animal mutations, winged abominations, and grotesque creatures that are operating worldwide, hiding within the velvet shadows of day and night, waiting patiently for the opportunity . . . to strike!

You hold in your hands the one object that terrifies even these gruesome ghouls! This book is the monster hunter's "bible." It explains in detail who these blood-chilling, satanic creatures are: their descriptions, cribs, strengths, powers, weaknesses, and fear factor!

We highlight the weapons, spells, equipment, and techniques you'll need to combat these maniacal monstrosities and survive the encounter!

You'll hear stories and relive experiences of monster hunters from present and past. Such as thirteen-year-old Tobias Toombes, who runs a slick monster-hunt blog! The diary of Australian schoolgirl Soul-Gon McDonald! Hands-on exclusives from intrepid reporter Neela Nightshade! Entries from the journals of the sixteenth-century monk Brother Jacob! And so much more!

Don't be shy! (A shy monster hunter—that's a good one!) We want to hear *your* stories of hunting these creepoids! Your successes and (hopefully few) failures! (Let's face it—if you lose a fight with a demon, at least you won't be around to die from embarrassment.)

Send us your reports, photos, artwork, blogs, tweets, diary and journal entries, film recordings, scrapbook pages, and other pertinent information regarding your battles with monsters, and your own ingenious methods for capturing and killing them.

Make your own Monster Fear Factor Top Ten list. Disagree with our assessments. Which monsters do *you* consider the scariest? (And for that matter, the dorkiest!) We love a good argument!

Monster hunting is awesome! And scary! And bloody! And sure, you probably won't live to see old age, but who wants to be a wrinkly prune anyhow?!

So grab your holy water, rosary beads, wooden stakes, and magic amulets, and let's go monster hunting!

DISCLAIMER: Anyone who goes monster hunting does so at their own risk. We cannot be held responsible for our readers turning into vampires, werewolves, zombies, or other assorted nasties.

TABLE OF CONTENTS

DEMONS

Hell is empty and all the devils are here.

—William Shakespeare—playwright and poet (1564-1616)

Ole Willy sure got that right!

Demons have been messing with humans ever since *Homo ergaster* first appeared in southern Africa during the early Pleistocene era, between 1.3 and 1.8 million years ago!

(FYI: *Homo* is the genus—the category—of great apes, which includes modern humans. *Homo ergaster* is believed to be the first species of early humans and the direct ancestor of subsequent human types such as *Homo heidelbergensis* [400,000–600,000 years ago]; *Homo neanderthalensis* [350,000–600,000 years ago]; and *Homo sapiens* [us lot!], 200,000 years ago. There is still some confusion as to whether *Homo erectus*—300,000–1.8 million years ago—is simply another name for *Homo ergaster* or a distinct species of its own. Those paleontologists! They can never agree on anything!)

Similar to humans, there are many different categories of demons: from the low-level kooky squirts such as Titivillus (the spelling demon) and Nybbas (inventor of the television and the World Wide Web—we kid you not!) to the terrifying, Japanese neck-stretching demoness Rokurokubi.

Depending upon the demon concerned, they are either fallen angels or those created by all the hate and evil in hell, and who are now working for the Great Granddaddy of Wickedness himself—Satan! (Or Shaitan, Iblis, Azazil, Jahannam, or Mara, depending upon your religious beliefs. We try to name-check them all!)

Then there are demons from other dimensions and planes of existence that have broken through into our reality, and those that have always existed here on Earth.

Whatever their gang colors, these are extremely powerful supernatural nasties who have but one goal—the utter extermination of the human race.

And their number is legion. These malignant, bloodletting, soul-stealing creatures are *everywhere*! Which, let's face it, is great news for us monster hunters because it means more demon butt-kicking action for us.

But hold your horses! It would be extremely remiss (and downright criminal) of us not to give fair warning to anyone who dreams of becoming a demonologist (someone who researches and combats demons).

From the moment you tangle with your first demon (and *if* you survive the encounter!) you'll be marked for life. Every demon that exists will be out to get you, no matter how long it takes.

From then on, while you think that you're hunting demons, they'll be hunting *you*! (But let's face it, if you wanted a boring, mundane life, you wouldn't be reading this book!)

Luckily, you have us to help prepare you for the bloody battles to come! In the following pages, you will meet some of the most gruesome and horrifying demons that ever oozed from the darkness!

Terrifying the good folk of the Middle East countries, we have the death-dealing abomination known as Pazuzu, who can lay waste to an entire country with but a single breath.

From Indonesia, the monstrous Buta Kala, who's to blame for everything bad in the world! (Yep, even reality TV shows! *Especially* reality TV shows! Ugh!)

The Alpine countries serve up Krampus, Santa's evil counterpart!

There's the psychotic Lady Midday, the water demon Davy Jones, the nightmare-inducing Bogeyman, and umpteen more!

For newbie monster hunters, we've even thrown in a few goofy ones to start you off. (Aww, c'mon! If you can't defeat the demon Abbasy, you definitely aren't in the right line of work! Cancel your membership to the International Federation of Monster Hunters—immediately.)

WATCH OUT!

THE AKANAME'S ABOUT!

Ministry of Health, Labor, and Welfare

'Fess up, guys! Who among us hasn't been in the bathroom standing over the toilet bowl, having a much-needed pee when a little tiny drop or two has splashed onto the floor? Who bothers to wipe that up, right?

We can hear all the girls going, "*Ewww*, disgusting!" but you're no better. Remember the times you've honked a mucous-thick green booger into a tissue and carelessly tossed it into the wastebasket, knowing it wouldn't be emptied for at least a week?

Does anyone scrub the soap scum from your bath or shower after washing? Flush away the loose hair, toe jam, and belly-button fluff? We're betting not often!

And let's not forget that humans have roughly 1.6 trillion skin cells (depending upon your size) that make up the epidermis (the outside skin layer, i.e., your body's overcoat).

Doesn't matter whether you're a kid or an adult, 30,000 to 40,000 of them fall off *every hour*! Over a twenty-four-hour period, you lose around one million skin cells, and your entire epidermis regrows approximately every twenty-seven to thirty days.

Over the course of an average life span, humans shed approximately 800 "skins," 105 pounds worth of the stuff, which is the weight of an average eleven-year-old child! That's a lot of flaked-off skin lying around.

Guess what? All this is how revolting germs and bacteria originate.

Luckily, there's a bright-red Japanese demon who loves all this stuff. The grimier and dirtier a bathroom and toilet are, the better.

The Akaname (垢嘗 in Japanese *kanji* script—yeah, we know, cool!) is a seriously freaky demon from Yomi (aka Yomi no Kuni), the Japanese name for the land of the dead (i.e., the underworld), which translates to *world of darkness*.

Hygiene is important for health and healthy living, but most humans don't bother to clean up properly once they've finished flushing the smelly waste products outta their systems. (We're lookin' at *you*, buddy!)

But if your mom complains about your unhygienic habits, tell her that cleaning the bathroom is sooo yesterday. The Akaname will do it for you.

His name literally means *filth licker*, and he does exactly that.

When night descends and everyone is asleep, the Akaname appears! Sticking out his elongated disease-riddled tongue, he *licks up* all the dirt, germs, and bacteria-causing organisms that humans have carelessly discarded.

The Akaname first appeared during Japan's Edo period (aka Tokugawa period, 1603–1867) when most Japanese visited a *sento*—a communal bathhouse—to clean themselves. (Yep, you'd get totally naked in front of strangers! It was all the rage back then. Go figure.)

Akaname was seen so often and became so famous that he even appeared in a short story collection from the period called *Kokon Hyaku Monogatari Hyōban*, about a demon who lives in public baths and dilapidated houses.

His celeb status was made real when he had a starring role in the first volume of scholar and artist Toriyama Sekien's best-selling *e-hon* (picture book) series, *Gazu Hyakki Yagyō* (*The Illustrated Night Parade of a Hundred Demons*), published in 1776. This is the series that really put the Japanese tsunami of *yōkai* (supernatural monsters) on the map. Way to go, Aka!

Case Study 833/89A

Kodomo (子供たち)—the Japanese word for children—are taught at an early age to keep

their bodies free of germs. The Ministry of Health, Labor, and Welfare recently released

a series of health posters and booklets for kindergarteners, encouraging kids to wash

properly. (Don't worry, we've translated this one for you!)

洗うこと

WASH

Ministry of Health, Labor, and Welfare

Konnichiha kodomo! (Hello Children!) Washing hands often and properly helps to prevent horrible diseases.

A naughty child who does not WASH! WASH! WASH! runs the risk of attracting the terrifying filth demon— _AKANAME!_

Follow these simple rules and BE SAFE!

Germs are EVERYWHERE! Everything you touch has germs! Your family! Your friends! Your pets! Your toys! So WASH! WASH! WASH! those hands! _OR AKANAME WILL GET YOU!_

Dirt attracts germs! So WASH! WASH! WASH! before eating! And after toileting or blowing your nose or playing outside WASH! WASH! WASH! again! _OR AKANAME WILL GET YOU!_

Lather up well when you WASH! WASH! WASH! Rub this lather hard over your palms and between your fingers and around your fingernails for at least ten seconds in warm running water! _OR AKANAME WILL GET YOU!_

Dry your little hands properly on a clean cloth or paper towel. And throw the used paper towel in the trash can! _OR AKANAME WILL GET YOU!_

If you MUST use a public toilet, DO NOT sit on the toilet seat! It will be INFESTED with germs! Squat over the bowl to perform your bodily duties! Afterward, flush away that soiled toilet paper! Then WASH! WASH! WASH! WASH! WASH! your hands before leaving the bathroom! _OR AKANAME WILL GET YOU!_

HAVE FUN! STAY SAFE! SLEEP WELL!

Published by the Ministry of Health, Labor, and Welfare

AKANAME FACT FILE

Location: Japan
Appearance: Diseased, rotting red body and elongated tongue; long, lank hair
Strength: Can lick a bathroom clean in a single night!
Weaknesses: Can't resist anything revolting, disgusting, and downright icckk!
Powers: Can make small kids wash their hands
Fear Factor: 97.4 (If you're a four-year-old! Anyone older than that: 6.1!)

WHAT TO DO WITH A CAPTURED AKANAME

AKANAME
Commercial & Residential Cleaning

Set up a cleaning company and hire out its services!

BATIBAT

A
C.B.I. Agent's
guide
to the
Philippines

-CBI-

Meet the Batibat (aka Bangungot), a vengeful demoness from the Philippines.

Taking the form of a grotesque, mugly (mondo-ugly), obese, wrinkly old woman, she delights in killing her victims in their sleep by sitting on their faces or chests with her huge, wobbly bottom cheeks.

Batti is so corpulent (incredibly overweight) that her victims cannot draw enough breath to shout for help, and slowly suffocate to death.

Thankfully, the majority of Filipinos have no worries. Batibat marks for death only young guys from the Ilocano people (aka Ilokano or Samtoy, from the Ilocano phrase *"sao mi ditoy,"* which translates as "our language here"). They mostly inhabit the island of Luzon, the largest in the Philippines.

With more than nine million people, the Ilocano make up 10.1 percent of the Filipino population.

Ole Batti is a committed environmentalist who lives a solitary and peaceful existence in the branches of trees. Leave her precious trees alone and she'll leave you alone. Her terrible anger falls only upon those who dare to mess with nature!

If a bedpost or frame of your house is made from deforested timber, the Batibat is going to get you!

Shrinking to bug size, she slips into the cracks of a felled tree. Once the timber has been turned into a home or bedroom furnishings, the Batibat waits for any boy or young man in the house to fall asleep before emerging. Then—she strikes!

When the lifeless body is discovered the next morning, doctors wrongly diagnose the cause of death as *bangungot* (nightmares)—yes, the disease has the same name as Batibat herself! It is also known as sudden unexpected nocturnal death syndrome (SUNDS), the sudden unexpected death of adolescents and young adults in their sleep.

Approximately 430 Filipinos die each year from Batibat's dread revenge! Our advice? Stop chopping down those trees. Otherwise, expect death to come a-knockin' on your bedroom door!

Or, in the immortal words of that great bard, Willie Shakespeare:

> To die, to sleep;
> to sleep: perchance to dream:
> aye, there's the rub;
> for in that sleep of death what dreams may come . . .
> *(Hamlet—written c.1603)*

CASE STUDY 557/63B

The following report was obtained under the Freedom of Information Act. It was filed by an agent of the Central Bureau of Investigation, the clandestine government agency that investigates all paranormal sightings. Dates, names, and specific locations have been redacted to protect the innocent.

CENTRAL BUREAU OF INVESTIGATION

Rock Hardy

THIS CERTIFIES THAT THE SIGNATURE AND PHOTOGRAPH HEREON IS AN APPROVED

SPECIAL AGENT

Case No: 33I/98B

████████, Republic of the ██████
████████ March 20██

The Pacific Ring of Fire is a 25,000-mile horseshoe-shaped basin in the Pacific Ocean. It holds 452 active and dormant volcanoes—more than 75 percent of the world's total—and 90 percent of the world's earthquakes and 8I percent of the largest earthquakes happen here. Scary stuff!

This agent has come to Luzon, the largest island of the Republic of the Philippines, one of the countries that make up the Ring, to investigate the deaths of a large number of male juvies and young men who appear to have been smothered in their sleep!

C.B.I. Agent's guide to the Philippines

Manila

Luzon

Palawan

17

The authorities suspect a female "supernatural" being they call the Batibat, who supposedly sits on her victim to kill him! The agent surmises a more plausible answer: A deranged serial killer is on the loose!

The agent stakes out ███████, one of the villages from which these attacks originated. It is the hot, dry summer season, lasting from March to May, and the air is stifling. Sweat quickly soaks through the agent's suit. Thankfully, the agent has been trained in the art of stealth suffering. The agent will not crack under any torture, not even the wearing of soggy underwear!

Night descends, and the agent's acute hearing makes out a loud rustling in the branches above him. Before the agent can react, the agent catches a glimpse of a blobulous mass hurtling down from above.

The ground violently shakes, and the agent is struck down by a sharp blow to the head. His senses reeling, the agent hears a terrified scream from inside a hut before darkness envelops him.

Upon recovering, the agent realizes that dawn has broken. Sobbing and wailing assaults his ears. The village is in an uproar. Another young man has died in his sleep. "Batibat!" the villagers cry in terror. "Batibat!"

The agent notices a number of large coconuts lying at his feet. A mild earthquake must have occurred last night, causing said coconuts to descend at a rapid rate upon the agent's head, knocking him unconscious. The young man, terrified at being awoken during an earthquake, was quite simply scared to death.

Of the so-called Batibat, the agent found no evidence of her existence. As per agreement with Regional Supervisor ████████████, the agent respectfully suggests that this case be closed, and not be presented to the relevant authorities on paranormal activities.

WHAT TO DO WITH A BATIBAT

Use her as the "Before" image for a slimming magazine.

BATIBAT FACT FILE

Location: Island of Luzon, Republic of the Philippines
Appearance: Gargantuan woman
Strength: Crushing!
Weaknesses: To scare away a Batibat, one must bite one's thumb or wiggle one's toe while asleep. (And the obvious drawback to this cunning plan is . . . ?)
Powers: Shape-shifter, fat attack
Fear Factor: 85.7 (if you're Ilocano; otherwise, party on, dude!)

*"The **Bogeyman** will get you if you don't watch out!"*

Chilling words spoken in whispered dread to terrified young children the world over.

Since time immemorial, the Bogeyman (aka Bogieman, Boogieman, Boogeyman, Bogleman, and Boogleman) has been preying on the young.

A shape-shifting demon of immense magical power, it takes delicious pleasure in terrorizing, kidnapping, murdering, eating, and/or decapitating little kids who misbehave.

The term is used metaphorically (as a figure of speech), for the Bogeyman can take any form: male, female, human, animal, mineral, or vegetable. Whatever spooks you most is the guise in which the Bogeyman will delightedly appear. (So if the thought of a giant purple carrot in a pink tutu dancing the fandango scares the bejeebers outta you, that's likely what you'll see!)

FRIENDS! ROMANS! COUNTRYMEN! LEND ME YOUR FEARS!

WITH THANKS TO WILLY SHAKESPEARE FOR THE INSPIRATION

Demonologists suspect that the Bogeyman has been petrifying kids and feasting on their innermost fears as far back as the reign of Augustus (31 BC–AD 14), the first Roman emperor—and probably earlier still.

Ancient Roman celeb poet Virgil (Publius Vergilius Maro, to give the dude his full title; 70 BC–19 BC) mentions such demons in his works. Virgil's poems were later translated from Latin by Scottish bishop, translator, and poet Gavin Douglas in 1513.

In the introduction to Volume 13 of the *Bukes of Eneados*, Douglas writes, "*Of Brownyis and of Bogillis full is this Buke.*" ("Of Brownies and of Bogles full is this book.") *Bogle* is the Scottish word for both ghost and supernatural being, and came into being around 1505.

The Bogeyman is further mentioned in the Middle English dialects that were spoken in England during the late eleventh and late fifteenth centuries (known as the High and Late Middle Ages). These dialects disappeared from use around 1470.

Back then, the word for *bogey* was *bogge* or *bugge*, meaning "frightening spectre"—which was also the word for *bug*.

But the best news for monster hunters is that there are *hundreds* of Bogeymen worldwide! You can't step out of your front door without tripping over them!

There is a Bogeyman in Belgium (*Oude Rode Ogen*—Old Red Eyes) who devours any child who stays out after sundown. And in Egypt, *Abu Rigl Maslukha*—Man With Burnt Legs—who cooks and eats naughty kids!

Burma has the *Pashu Gaung Phyat*, meaning Headhunter. There's the *mörkö* of Finland; France's *Le Croque-Mitaine* (the Hand-Cruncher); and in Quebec, Canada, *Le Bonhomme Sept-Heures* (the Seven o'clock Man).

Not forgetting our particular favorites: Bloody Bones from the Southern US, and *Bubak* (aka *hastrman*) from the Czech Republic and Poland, who on the nights of a full moon weaves clothes for the children and adults he's kidnapped. And get this—he has a cart pulled by cats!

unsurprisingly, some kids grow up so scared of the Bogeyman that it messes with their head. There is a genuine anxiety disorder known as bogyphobia, the fear of the Bogeyman, which affects hundreds of kids and adults every year.

During our investigations, we have been given access to a recent psych report on a disturbed patient suffering from bogyphobia.

Psychiatric Assessment Medical Transcription

DATE OF CONSULTATION: 30 February ███████

IDENTIFICATION: This is a ███ year-old single male.

PRESENTING COMPLAINT: The patient reported history of agitation and stress, as well as hearing disembodied voices and "seeing things" in the shadows.

HISTORY OF PRESENT ILLNESS: Ever since the patient was three or four, his parents made him aware of a supernatural entity, which the patient identifies as "the Bogeyman." This "Bogeyman," he was repeatedly warned, would come in the night and steal him away if he did not behave. The older he grew, the worse the threats from the Bogeyman became. The child would be kidnapped, his parents told him. Then beaten. Tortured for days. Boiled in a cooking pot. Decapitated. And eaten.

The patient reported having extreme psychiatric problems since early childhood, but doctors could not diagnose what caused them. He had a difficult adolescence, with bed-wetting, depression, and screaming fits being the norm.

His present condition includes audio and visual hallucinations, rambling speech, and lack of concentration. He believes the Bogeyman is coming for him. He sees the Bogeyman in every dark corner——hiding under his bed or behind the curtain——and hears the demon's rasping breath and cackling laugh coming from inside his closet.

DIAGNOSIS: The patient is clearly deranged, with an antisocial personality disorder. This imaginary friend, "the Bogeyman," is clearly his mind's attempt to revert back to happier times of his young childhood.

TREATMENT PLAN: The patient needs to be immediately placed in a padded room of the local psychiatric hospital. Removal of all sharp objects is advised, as is his being placed in a straitjacket for his own good.

RECOMMENDATIONS: This patient is a long-term health risk, both to himself and others, and in my professional evaluation, should never be released.

Dr. U. R. Nutz MD, MPH, DFAPA, FACP, FRCP, PQRST, UV, WXYZ
Psychiatrist

HOW TO CATCH THE BOGEYMAN

Booby-trap a little kid's bedroom floor with quick-drying superglue. When the Bogeyman appears, its feet will stick fast! (Unless the kid's idea of the Bogeyman is a murderous, intangible green mist—then you do have problems!)

BOGEYMAN FACT FILE

Location: Everywhere
Appearance: Whatever scares you the most
Strength: As powerful as a kid's imagination allows it to be
Weaknesses: The demon is a sucker for Nervous Nellie kids
Powers: Can turn little kids into quivering wrecks
Fear Factor: 99.9

Avast there, ye scurvy bilge rats! Batten down th' hatches! If it be th' nautical demon Davy Jones ye be after, th' Scourge o' th' Seven Seas we say, then it be time t'get yer feet wet! But beware, me hearties! For dead men tell no tales! Oh, arrrh! Yo ho ho! Pieces of eight!

Pardon our embarrassing impersonation of a sixteenth-century pirate captain, but when discussing such a subject as Davy Jones, it's kind of a done deal.

Succinctly described by Scottish poet and writer Tobias Smollet (1721–1771) in his novel *The Adventures of Peregrine Pickle* (published in 1751), Davy Jones totally owns the world's seabeds. He is *"the fiend that presides over all the evil spirits of the deep."*

A popular misconception is that Davy Jones is human, possibly the ghost of a sailor drowned at sea. Wrong! He's a full-fledged demon, a shape-shifter of some note who changes his appearance upon the whims of the tide. One day, a blue devil with horns and tail, the next, a skeletal figure with glowing eyes in a pirate's costume.

Ten thousand years ago in the Middle East, some inventive Neolithic dude had the bright idea of hollowing out a fallen tree trunk using stone tools. He fastened an animal skin sail to a tall pole in the middle and laughingly called it a sailing vessel—the very first of its kind. Since that momentous day, the diabolic Davy Jones has been merrily sending unwary sailors on a one-way trip to a watery grave.

DJ really came into his own around 3000 BC, when the ancient Egyptians figured out how to lash planks together with woven straps, and seal the seams with reeds and grass to form a hull. And thus, man's conquest of the oceans finally began.

And Davy Jones was waiting to greet them!

It doesn't matter whether a vessel is made from wood or steel. With prodigious strength, Davy will simply smash through its hull.

Possessing omnipotent elemental powers, he can create terrible storms, herding ships until they smash onto submerged rocks or into drifting icebergs or else capsize them, dragging all those aboard down to Davy Jones's Locker! (DJ's "locker" is a seabed graveyard of drowned sailors and pirates, whose tormented souls are trapped therein forevermore!)

Davy Jones's celeb status was sealed when English writer, journalist, trader, and—get this!—spy Daniel Defoe (1660–1731; he of *Robinson Crusoe* fame) first referenced the seafaring devil in his 385-page story *The Four Years Voyages of Captain George Roberts* (1726).

And ole Davy continues drowning unwary sailors to this very day!

CASE STUDY 889/5DJ

A Maritime Board of Inquiry was held after the sinking of the oceanographic research vessel *Unsinkable* in the freezing waters of the East Siberian Sea off the coast of Pevek, Russia. Positioned above the Arctic Circle and with an average daytime high temperature of -12.3 °F/-24.6 °C, there were sadly no survivors.

Here follows a transcript of the distress call received by Pevek Maritime Rescue from the *Unsinkable* call sign WOAH that was released at the coroner's inquest.

MR—Maritime Rescue UP—Unknown person

Unsinkable: *SOS CQ DE WOAH——Unsinkable at 0800 GMT. Vessel down by* [distorted]. *We are being attacked! I repeat* [distorted]——*by terrifying* [distorted] *from the ocean depths! POSN 69°42'N 170°17'E—MASTER + Need assistance! Any vessels in the area please* [distorted] [crackles]

Maritime Rescue: Pevek Maritime Rescue Station calling. Please repeat your message. Over.

Unsinkable: [crackles] *Thank Go——yes, this is* Unsinkable [sounds of screams in background]. *You copy? Over.*

MR: *Unsinkable, this is Pevek Maritime Rescue reading you loud and clear. Go ahead. Over.*

Unsinkable: *We have an emergency situ*[crackles]——. *Our vessel* [sounds of gunshots, screaming] *overrun by hideous humanoid* [loud screams]——. *There are dozens of th*[screams, rapid gunfire] *climbing up the side of the hul*[distorted]——. *They are kill*[screams] *on board! Someone, please, hel*[distorted]——

MR: *Unsinkable, it sounds like you're having a real kickin' party on board. Over.*

Unsinkable: *For pity's sake! Listen! Their bodies are rotting flesh and skelet*[rapid gunfire]——. *Their eyes are burning flames! My crew is being hacked dow*[screams, gunshots]——*Please, someone! HELP US!!* [distorted]

MR: *Unsinkable, please remember maritime radio communications rules and regulations. Please say over when finished speaking. Over.*

Unsinkable: *You idiot! We need assis*[crackle]——*wait! There's someone coming into the cabin! I——* [loud gasp] [to unknown person] *Wh- who are you?!*

UP: [rasping voice, echoing] *Humans have named me Davy Jones! The fools! I am* [distorted], *high demon of the Seventh Level of He*[explosions, screams, rapid gunfire]. *Anyone who sails upon my seas must pay the ultimate penalty! Death!*

Plate 16 - Davy Jones

Unsinkable: *No! No! Keep back! Keep [crackles]— aaaaaaaah!! [distorted silence]*

MR: *Unsinkable, please speak more clearly. Are you saying that you have an emergency situation on board? [silence] Unsinkable? [silence] Do you copy? Over.*

[silence]

MR: *I repeat, do you copy? Over.*

[silence]

MR: *Unsinkable, do you copy? Over.*

[Continues to call Unsinkable with no response.]

HOW TO CAPTURE DAVY JONES

1. Build a ship in a large bottle made of tempered glass. (Extremely strong glass.)
2. Place it on the seabed at Davy Jones's last known position.
3. Unable to resist, the demon will shrink in size and swim into the bottle to attack the vessel.
4. Swim out from your hiding place behind a rock and seal Davy Jones inside the bottle with a tight-fitting cork. Gotcha!

DAVY JONES FACT FILE

Location: The world's ocean depths
Appearance: He's a shape-shifter
Strength: Demonic
Weaknesses: Can't resist singing sea shanties on karaoke night
Powers: Weather control, shape-shifting
Fear Factor: 52.7

Ever daydreamed of finding an old lamp, giving it a quick rub, and out pops a genie to grant you three wishes? Well, try it with these Arabian supernatural nasties and they're likely to turn you into a thick, rancid puddle of goo.

According to the Koran, the ancient religious text of Islam, the jinn (aka djinn) first appeared on Earth about two thousand years before humans first made their stumbling, accident-prone appearance. Allah (the Arabic word for *God*) created the angels, the jinn, and humans.

As is quoted in the Koran (which was written between 609–632 by the prophet Muhammad), Allah said: "*I did not create the jinn and mankind except to worship Me.*" (Koran 51:56)

And like us humans, there are good, bad, and indifferent jinn. The three main jinn baddies are the Amir (aka Aamir), who pops into someone's home for a cappuccino and completely forgets to leave, making a pesky nuisance of itself; the much more psycho and wicked Shaytan; and the Ifrit, who are even more powerful and vicious than the Shaytan. (We'd give these a miss if we were you!)

Created by Allah in a smokeless and scorching fire, the jinn (singular: jinni) live mostly in a parallel dimension to our own. That said, many jinn reckon that Earth is kind of cool and so hang out in deserts and wastelands, on mountains, under the sea, inside trees and rocks, in cemeteries and ruins, and inside trash cans. Some even visit the demon Akaname in the john (We kid you not!).

These guys and gals (yep, there are female jinn) have some mojo powers including magic, invisibility (the word *jinn* in Arabic means "hidden from sight"), flying, super-speed, body-snatching, and shape-shifting! And yes, jinn really can grant wishes!

In the words of Ibn Taymiyyah (1263–1328), the Islamic scholar, theologian (religious expert), and logician (a person skilled at logic), the jinn can take on any form they like: human, animal, or object. He described them as typically "*ignorant, untruthful, oppressive and treacherous.*"

Three useful ways to protect yourself from a jinni attack are to leave out food and charcoal to keep it friendly; ask permission before turning on the tap (because some sneaky jinn hide in water pipes); and sprinkle salt on the floor around your bed before zzzzzzz-time!

CASE STUDY 538/01J

The British Museum in London, England, was founded in 1753 and first opened its doors to the public on January 15, 1759. It holds the world's largest collection of human antiquities, charting our culture and development from the very dawn of mankind.

One piece acquired by the museum was recently featured on its website. Strangely, moments after being uploaded, the page mysteriously disappeared—but not before we had Ctrl C & V'd the report, which we reproduce below.

Research News

The 24.5-centimeter, ten-inch brass lamp was discovered during an archaeological dig at caves in the Zagros Mountains in the Kurdistan region of the Republic of Iraq. These caves are close to the famous Shanidar Cave, where skeletal remains of Neanderthals dating back sixty to eighty thousand years were excavated between 1957 and 1961.

The lamp has been carbon dated to the seventh or eighth century BC, a time when the people of Assyria (a kingdom in northern Mesopotamia, present-day Iraq) first began smelting zinc-rich copper ore from the rocks.

It was found resting on top of a large slab of rock in the center of the cave. Australian archaeologist Professor Diggum Upp later revealed that upon seeing the lamp, he felt an uncanny urge to "give the li'l ripper a rub, fair dinkum!"

Upon doing so, Upp claims that a greenish-blue ethereal smoke poured out from the spout of the lamp, filling up the cave "like a cow's fart in a balloon, I reckon!"

Upp further claims that the smoke transformed into the shape of a giant blue humanoid figure, whose voice bellowed out: "Mortal, I am jinn. You have released me from my prison. I must grant you three wishes." Upp said that his mind whirled with the possibilities. He was "as happy as a fox in a chook house!"

"I'm waiting!" bellowed the apparition, swirling angrily around Upp. Frustrated, Upp replied, "I wish ya would stay still, ya silly drongo!" The jinn stopped moving.

"Two wishes!" it bellowed.

"Noo!" Upp cried out. "I wish I hadn't said that! Oops!"

The jinn bellowed a third time: "One wish!"

Upp then lost his temper and shouted, "Oooh! I wish ya'd just disappear, ya yobbo!"

Other members of the team found Upp some hours later. He was sitting in the cave, clutching the lamp and frantically rubbing it, calling out, "Come back, ya blodger! Come back!"

Upp has now been relieved of his duties.

HOW TO DESTROY JINN

These guys aren't loaded with brains, so if one attacks, challenge it to shape-shift into a goldfish—then feed it to the cat!

JINN FACT FILE

Location: The world, although mostly Arabic countries

Appearance: A tree, a rock, your teach, a booger . . .

Strength: Magical

Weaknesses: Oooh, lots! Imprisoning the jinn in a brass lamp or lead-stoppered bottle, wearing a magic talisman, throwing the pit of a fruit at it, taking seven hairs from an all-black cat (except for a white tip on its tail) and burning the hairs in a small, closed room . . . you know, the usual stuff!

Powers: Magic, invisibility, body-hopping and possession, flight, super-speed, super-strength, shape-shifting

Fear Factor: 46 (in human/animal form); 76.4 (in jinn form)

Move aside, Santa, ya weight-challenged wobble-butt! Ya saccharine sweet cutie pie, Christmas days are over! No more crass commercialism cunningly disguised as a sacred religious festival for us.

Meet Krampus, aka Dark Santa! Best described as Santa Claus's most badassical alter ego, Krampus believes that terror, torture, and violent murders are much more fun presents to give naughty kids at Christmas!

Hitching a ride on Santa's sleigh each Christmas Eve, Krampus delights in following through on Santa's own pathetically feeble threats to punish naughty tykes—you know that "not giving them presents" bologna! Oooh, scary!—with his own style of truly gruesome punishments.

Like what, you ask? Like pulling disobedient punks outta their homes by their hair and savagely thrashing them with either a birch stick, barbed whip, or rusty chain until they lie whimpering and bleeding on the snow-covered ground!

And if he's in a particularly foul mood, he'll rip out little girls' pigtails or clamp kids in shackles before leading them off a cliff! Sickly.

Kids who have messed up big-time will be stuffed into his sack or in a washtub strapped to Krampus's back, and then carted off for either a drowning, a devouring, or to be dragged screaming to the fiery pits of hell itself!

And for *really* bad little snots, he pushes their faces into a deep pool of ink and holds them there until they drown! Then he stabs a sharp pitchfork through their corpses to lift them out again! News flash! Krampus is way older than Santa, who first appeared in the guise of Greek Bishop Nicholas (AD 270–343), a seriously cool guy who used to leave coins and gifts for poor people and was rightly canonized (declared a saint) for his work, which is why today's Santa has the tag Saint Nick.

Predating Christianity by a few thousand years, Krampus was already well established in Alpine pagan celebrations. (Pagans do not follow organized religions like Christianity, Judaism, or Islam. They prefer to worship nature and may worship many gods or none.)

His Old High German name (Old High German is the earliest form of the German language and existed from AD 500–1050) was *Krampen*, meaning *claw*, and was the inspiration for our Santa's own additional name "Claus."

He's usually described as having razor-sharp claws; two massive, curved horns; cloven hooves; a monstrously long, pointed tongue; and a body covered in thick black or brown hair.

Across Europe, the Feast of Saint Nicholas is celebrated every December 6 in memory of Bishop Nicholas. But an even more bodacious party is held the night before in honor of Krampus!

On *Krampusnacht* (Krampus Night), partygoers dress up as devils, demons, wild men, and witches before participating in the "Krampus Run," which basically means running through the streets of the city screaming and hollering, ringing bells and blowing horns, and scaring the sweet bejeebers out of fellow citizens! Go, Krampus!

CASE STUDY 099/54K

Thirteen-year-old monster hunter Tobias Toombes posts a weekly blog.

A MONSTER HUNTER'S BLOG

TRACKING, TRAPPING, AND DESTROYING THE THINGS THAT SHOULDN'T EXIST

FRIDAY DECEMBER 25

KRAMPUS

ABOUT ME

By day Tobias Toombes is a mild-mannered student; at night he hunts the creatures from your worst nightmare.

Blog Archive

Nachzehrer
Ankou
Tengu
Davy Jones
Banshees
Furies
Mothman
Ogopogo

'Tis the night before Crimbo, and a demon doth prowl
Snatchin' kids from their cribs with a screech and a howl
If youz were a bad 'un, 'tis time to fear and dread
'Cuz Krampus has brung ya a prezzie—he's gonna turn ya quite . . . DEAD!

Nice poem, eh? It's one I made up while trackin' down that demonic Xmas nasty beast known as KRAMPUS!

So it's da midnight hour of Crimbo Eve. The ground covered in thick snow. I'm dressed in my best winter togs, eyeballin' the pads in the super-swanky area o' town, when I see a red-suited figure, poppin' up and down chimneys and in and outta windows carrying a bulgin' sack. It's Santa, hard at work!

Moments after he departs, this hideous shape slithers from the darkness, speedily clamberin' up the side o' a three-story house! With hairy body, curved horns, cloven feet, and a tail, it ain't da Crimbo Fairy! The hellborn horror disappears through a bedroom window and *ticktock, ticktock*, is back out again, carrying a small bundle under its lanky arm.

Leapin' down, it lands hard, sprayin' snow, and I see Krampus in all his freaky-deak glory! The "bundle" is a little brat o' about six, who's a-screamin' and a-wailin' in heart-stoppin' terror!

"Out of my way, child!" growls Krampus in a sibilant hiss, his lollin' tongue air-walkin' in front o' me!

Monster hunters are brave (kinda) but we ain't stoopid. I know I have no chance o' beatin' this mugly dude, but neither is he takin' the kid!

So I do the only thing possible! I lift up a large rock and heave it . . . but not at Krampus! It flies over his head and——SMAAASSH! The kid's downstairs window explodes! Alarm bells start a-ringin', lights come on across da 'hood, and Krampus knows when he's beaten!

Dropping the tyke, he scampers away! "Next year, child!" he snarls, the darkness swallowin' him up. "I come——for *you*!"

Yeah, Kramps! Good luck with that!

Oh, and that "Santa" I eyeballed? Turns out he was a burglar! He wasn't deliverin' presents, he was stealin' 'em! Oops!

KRAMPUS FACT FILE

Location: The Alpine countries (Slovenia, Austria, Switzerland, Liechtenstein, Germany, France, Italy, and Monaco); the United States

Appearance: Hairy demon with horns and cloven feet; scary dude in black clothes

Strength: Thinks Santa's a wimp!

Weaknesses: Loves to party!

Powers: Shape-shifter. The power to terrify little boogers into behaving!

Fear Factor: 0 (little angels); 100 (bad kids)

BEST USE OF KRAMPUS

I. Make a list of all the bad stuff your bratty little brother or sister/worst enemy gets up to during the year, and send it to Krampus! They'll never bother you again!

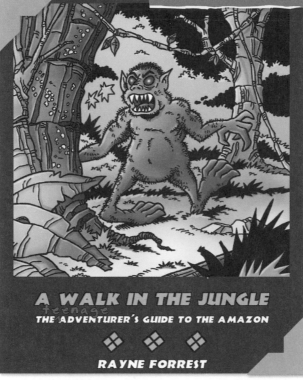

A WALK IN THE JUNGLE
THE ADVENTURER'S GUIDE TO THE AMAZON

❖ ❖ ❖

RAYNE FORREST

This Amazonian demon saves his hideous wrath (we aren't kidding!) for those twisted individuals who hunt animals for "sport" or who kill more animals than they can possibly eat or carry.

A totally committed animal activist, Kuru-Pira (aka Curupira) is also the protector of the Desana and Tupí-Guaraní people of the Amazon rainforest.

These tribes can be found living along the Rio Negro (the world's largest "blackwater" river, which is a slow-moving river flowing through forests, swamps, and wetlands), which cuts through both Colombia and Brazil.

A shape-shifter, Kuru-Pira can take many forms, most notably a paca, a brocket deer, a frog, or a young boy with body blisters and flaming red hair.

His favorite disguise is that of a short, ugly, hairy creature with red, burning eyes and sharp fangs. His ears are pointed and stand erect, and he has no knee joints. And his oversized long feet face backward!

Kuru-Pira's footprints confuse the frightened hunters. Thinking that they show where Kuru-Pira has just come from, the hunters dash off in the opposite direction to escape his terrible vengeance—only to hurtle headlong into his unbreakable grasp!

Leaping upon his prey, Kuru-Pira lets out his distinctive battle growl: *"Boraro!"* Once seized, there is no escape! Kuru-Pira has two favorite methods of dispatch: He will either urinate over his victim, instantly burning all flesh from their bones (surprisingly, this *isn't* the disgusting part!), or else he'll crush out their life with his bare hands!

Once they're dead, the demon will drill a small hole in the victim's head and suck out not only the blood but *all the flesh and bone*, leaving an empty bag of skin!

Once his meal is finished, he closes up the hole and blows up the skin like a balloon. The reanimated corpse now serves as Kuru-Pira's zombified servant, helping to protect the animals from other hunters!

CASE STUDY 587/4KK

Fourteen-year-old British girl Rayne Forrest's parents are members of the Explorers Club, an international society founded in New York City in 1904. Past members include Robert Peary, Matthew Henson, and Ootah (first to reach the North Pole, in 1909); Roald Amundsen (first to reach the South Pole, in 1911); Sir Edmund Hillary and Tenzing Norgay (first to reach the summit of Mount Everest, the world's highest peak, in 1953); and Neil Armstrong, Buzz Aldrin, and Michael Collins (first to reach the surface of the moon, in 1969).

For summer break, Rayne's mom and dad took her trekking through the Amazon (as one does). Rayne kept a journal of her expedition, which will soon be published under the title *A Walk in the Jungle*.

Here is an exclusive excerpt from that book:

Day 57

We're, like, *deep* in the forest now, camping near one of the tributary rivers. Everyone else is having a snooze, but I can't sleep. My head's half-gaga with the *majesty* of this place! Outside my tent, there's this never-ending cacophony of shrieks and growls from the jungle inhabitants who are getting stroppy about us trespassing on their turf.

Dad tells me that while the Amazon may be the largest tropical rainforest left on Earth, covering 2.5 million square miles, at the rate we dumb humans are destroying it there will be NO RAINFOREST LEFT in thirty-five years' time! One hundred fifty acres are being torn down *every* **minute!!**

This place is called "the lungs of the planet" for a reason. More than 20 percent of all the oxygen we breathe is produced here. Zip ahead forty years and there'll be eight billion humans breathing 20 percent less oxygen——good luck with that! *Grrr!!*

A loud rustling outside has me ear-wigging. Jaguar? Green anaconda? I'm trying not to freak out!

Tooling up with Dad's machete, I go outside for a look-see . . . and find a set of oversized human-like footprints leading away from the camp.

Sniffing a skanky foot pong, I spin around to find this freaky little hairy snot giving me the evil eye. And here's the kicker—if you'll pardon the pun—his feet are back-to-front!

Hell's bells! I suss it straight off. "Kuru-Pira!" (Our Desana guides had warned us about this spud ugly but we just laughed.)

"Whoa!" I stammer. His eyes blazing fiercely, the sad arse gets all lairy and screeches "*Boraro!*" before leaping at me!

Remembering the advice of our guides, I roll beneath him, slamming my hand in his footprint . . . and Kuru-Pira freezes where he lands! HEAVY!

"Right," say I, somewhat hacked off. "Enough of this guff. We're not gonna hurt you." I dig him lightly with the tip of the machete, his eyes registering understanding. "Got it?"

He got it! Now whenever I hear strange noises on our travels I know it's Kuru-Pira, keeping watch over us!

KURU-PIRA FACT FILE

Location: Amazon rainforest in Colombia and Brazil
Appearance: Short, fat, hairy guy; disgusting blistery ginger kid; all kinds of animals
Strength: Crushing!
Weaknesses: Push him over and he can't stand up (no knees); slap your hand in his footprint and he freezes; step in his track facing the opposite direction and Kuru-Pira's internal GPS navigation goes outta whack; running backward while staring him in the eyes will also confuse him!
Powers: Demonic strength, shape-shifter
Fear Factor: 49.6

WHAT TO DO WITH KURU-PIRA

Sell him as a test subject to an anti-foot odor manufacturer!

Summer's here, and the livin' is easy . . . except maybe if you're a kid out in the countryside sniffing the flowers, or a worker toiling in the fields under a blazing sun, because then death be a-stalkin' ya!

Death in the form of that diabolically demonic demoness—Lady Midday!

Lady M. (aka Pscipolnitsa, Poluudnica, Polednice, Poloznicha, Připołdnica, Přezpołdnica . . . anyway, lots of unpronounceable names beginning with the letter *P*!) has a major beef with people of Slavic descent.

There are roughly 350 million to 400 million Slavic people in the world, mostly hanging loose in Europe and Asia Minor. They are classified as either East Slavic, including Russians (the largest of the groups with more than 150 million people), Ukrainians, and Belarusians; West Slavic from the countries of Poland, the Czech Republic, and Slovakia; and South

Slavic, which consists of people from Macedonia, Slovenia, Croatia, and the like.

Okay, an extra fifty points if you know why this abominable apparition calls herself Lady Midday? Well, it isn't because she comes out at night. Lady M. roams the countryside during summer, appearing at midday (that wasn't difficult!) when both sun and heat are at their most intense.

POLICE SKETCH
A VISUAL DESCRIPTION OF THE SUSPECT

POLICE DEPARTMENT
Southern Federal District
Krasnodar Krai

ARTIST CIRCULAR
NO. 1782
RE PREPARED 09/08

LIMITED TO
DEPARTMENT
CIRCULATION

Sometimes she'll appear as a swirling dust cloud or whirlwind to choke any unfortunate soul who stands in her way. Other times, as a sweet and innocent twelve-year-old girl, or as an old hag with hairy legs.

Her über-favorite disguise is that of a stunningly beautiful young woman in a long, white dress. What's so scary about that, you ask? It's what she keeps hidden behind her back that you should worry about!

Calling out cheerily to sweat-soaked workers in a field, she engages them in friendly conversation, or she may perhaps ask them a seemingly innocent yet difficult question.

If they dare try to change subjects before Lady M. has finished speaking or flub the pop quiz, she flies into a satanic rage, whips out a deadly sharp scythe or large pair of farm shears, and—cuts off their head! *SNECK!*

Other ways of dispatching victims is by causing agonizing and death-dealing sunstroke, weakening their limbs so that they become bedridden, or else driving them mad.

And if she catches sight of a child happily playing, she will swoop down and steal away the terrified brat, who will never again be seen!

CASE STUDY 678/OLM

We've managed to "procure" (i.e., purchase with the aid of a wad of money and a plain brown envelope) a copy of a Russian politsiya—police—report concerning a recent attack by Lady Midday on farmworkers.

We've translated the report from the original Russian text. And hope that we don't get a surprise visit from the FSB—the Federalnaya Sluzhba Bezopasnosti, Russia's dreaded secret police!

At approximately 1307 hours on 9 August, I arrived at
the small farm of Mr. Ivor Boilonmybumkov, located in
the Southern Federal District of Krasnodar Krai.

The weather was abnormally hot. At noon, it reached
38°C, so I was in no mood to be investigating
nonsensical reports of a murder at the hands of a
"phantom woman."

Mr. Boilonmybumkov led me to the field where the
murder took place. Waiting for us were four farmhands
looking extremely nervous—or more probably,
guilty. They stood around the body of the victim. I
immediately noticed that his head was detached from
the body.

The farm manager, Mr. Ivan Alibi, was one of the
witnesses to the attack. "It was terrible!" he told me,
wringing his hands and perspiring in a guilty manner
in the oppressive heat. "We were working in the field
at noon precisely, when a dust cloud arose, as if from
nowhere. When it died away, a beautiful young lady in
a white dress appeared beside the fence."

The woman allegedly beckoned the men over to her.
They were all enjoying a friendly discourse when the
victim, Mr. Kanya Believeit, rudely interrupted her.

Immediately, the woman flew into a terrible rage.
Screaming abuse, she produced an oversized pair of
farming shears and snipped off Mr. Believeit's head.
Cackling madly, she disappeared once more in a swirl
of dust.

A likely story. I surmise that the farmhands had a
falling-out over some trivial reason—brought on by

mild sunstroke, no doubt; not one of the men was wearing protective headgear——and they turned on Mr. Believeit and murdered him.

I conducted a survey of the crime scene but found no evidence to support their wild claims. I then asked the workers to accompany me to the station to help compose a police sketch of the alleged attacker.

Once this was completed, I handed the terrified men over to the FSB. They will no doubt extract the truth from their dying breaths.

Tikally Koffkof

HOW TO CAPTURE LADY MIDDAY

When she turns into a dust cloud, spray her with water, turning her into gloopy mud!

LADY MIDDAY FACT FILE

Location: Europe and Asia Minor (aka the Anatolia peninsula. This comprises the Asian part of Turkey, and is surrounded by the Black Sea, the Aegean Sea, and the Mediterranean Sea.)

Appearance: Hot babe dressed all in white; old hag with unshaven legs; twelve-year-old girl; dust cloud/whirlwind combo

Strength: Psychotic human

Weaknesses: Cloudy days; any time after midday (so take a long lunch before confronting her!)

Powers: Shape-shifter, flight, razor-sharp scythe or pair of farm shears

Fear Factor: 63.1 (midday); 9.5 (any time after midday)

Lamiae (the plural of Lamia) have been munching down on munchkins and slurping down the blood of young men across Europe for thousands of years.

The original Lamia was either the daughter or granddaughter of Poseidon (the god of the sea), and mother to two totally grotesque sea monsters named Skylla and Akheilos.

Or she was a beautiful queen of ancient Libya, a country in northwest Africa, located in the Mediterranean Sea.

If you favor the latter version, then you kind of have to feel sympathy for Lamia, because her child-chomping ways were caused by Zeus (total-jerk god of the sky and thunder, and ruler of Mount Olympus), who took a fancy to her.

This enraged his wife Hera, who either stole away Lamia's children or forced her to eat them. *(Ooo-kaaayyy . . .)* This drove the poor woman understandably nutzoid, and in some sort of twisted revenge, Lamia has been enjoying a plate of *chili con child* ever since!

Shape-shifters, Lamia and her brethren have been variously described as being beautiful women with a giant serpent's tail below the waist, women with distorted faces (from eating too many children), stone gargoyles with large wingspans, or even three-headed dragon/hydra monsters!

They are also considered vampires who steal away little children and hypnotize young men so they may drink their blood.

And many Greeks believe the Lamiae to be ogresses who live in remote houses or towers deep in the forests or up on the mountains, and possess magical abilities.

Famous English poet John Keats (1795–1821) was so enamored by the story of Lamia that he wrote the demoness her own narrative poem for his book published in 1820, *Lamia, Isabella, The Eve of St. Agnes and Other Poems*. (Not noted for his short book titles, our John.)

But as a stone-hearted monster hunter who doesn't go in for this soppy *luuurrrvvve* stuff, you have your work cut out for you.

Luckily, there's some good news! The Lamiae may be vicious and deadly but they're also rather stupid. Even a member of the forty-watt club should be able to best one of these beasties. (And if you don't, hey, you won't be around to complain to us!)

CASE STUDY 209/67L

In 1534, English King Henry VIII (1491–1547) was "slightly peeved" with the Roman Catholic Church for not letting him get divorced, so he closed down all their religious buildings and persecuted the friars and monks thereof.

One Franciscan monk, Brother Jacob, decided to "get the heck outta Dodge" and left England to sail the globe. On his travels, he ran into Lamia at the Acropolis in Athens, Greece.

(FYI: Work started on building the Parthenon at the Acropolis of Athens in 447 BC and was completed nine years later. The term acropolis means "the highest point of the town." There you go! And we didn't even charge you extra for it!)

THE ADVENTURES OF BROTHER JACOB
"Get thee behind me, Satan!"

These exalted words of our Lord, the almighty creator, I did make utterance of in dire confrontation with the evil demoness Lamia!

Her serpentine body writhed high above me, blocking out the divine heaven's light that was created by the Infinite Spirit and that we mere mortals have named the sun.

Before I had time to prepare for battle, the vile villainess did make ready to strike!

Knoweth thee that upon my travels I have seen many wondrous sights. One such was a clay urn from the distant times of ancient Greece, which showed upon its face a form most monstrous in its appearance. The child-eater, Lamia!

And thus this Lord's servant did make haste by boat to the country that first developed understanding of all things.

Situated between the wooded Hill of the Nymphs and rocky Philopappos Hill, the Acropolis's mighty marble columns soared upward in stunning majesty!

Mere moments after mine arrival thereat, I espied a huge serpentine form in the shadows of the Great Place, one emanating such evil as to shatter my senses!

"Foolissssh human!" hissed Lamia, for that is who it was. "Get thee anon. I shalt but give thee one chance to depart!"

"Fierce me not so readily, foul fiend!" I cried, bringing forth my sacred sword and battle-ax. "Verily, thou must make thy peace with God before I send thy shriveled soul back from whence it came!"

It was while I was proclaiming Judgment Day upon Mephistopheles's mistress that she did attack!

With a priestly cry, I leapt to action, swinging hard my sword, which I have affectionately named Seraph!

Hissing angrily, Lamia struck ferociously again and again, attempting to rip out my throat with her deadly fangs! HSSSSSSS!

"God, I implore thee," I fervently prayed. "Grant me the power to destroy this wicked wretch!"

THUNK! Seraph struck home, piercing Lamia's leathery hide! Icy black blood gushed from her wound o'er me, and Lamia screamed her sweet death song! "Nyaaaaaaaaah!"

The towering form crashed mightily earthward. Kneeling to catch my spiritual breath, I glanced up to find that the Lamia——had *disappeared!* Taken by Satan no doubt, to burn for her failure in the fiery pits of hell and damnation! The Lord's work be done! Hallelujah!

HOW TO CATCH LAMIA

Hire a snake charmer to hypnotize Lamia into a giant-size basket. Seal the lid and you're good to go!

LAMIA FACT FILE

Location: North Africa and Europe
Appearance: Beautiful snake lady; three-headed dragon; stone gargoyle
Strength: Murderous!
Weaknesses: Rosemary and salt (yeah, we know, weird!). Cover Lamia with the stuff and then set it alight. Whoooossh! Stab her with a silver dagger blessed by a priest. Trap Lamia in a circle of crystals and perform a banishing spell. (So we hope your magical incantations are fully up-to-date and in working order!) Oh, and decapitation—that's always a good one!
Powers: Shape-shifter, bloodsucker. Immortal-ish.
Fear Factor: 74.1

Musée du Louvre

Assyrian demon Pazuzu
first millennium BC

Discover the work   1/4

Depending on which side of the bed he gets out of each morning, Pazuzu may be in a fire-and-brimstone foul temper and delight in raining down misery, despair, and death upon hapless humans.

Or else he'll feel extra-chirpy and fight off other evil spirits to protect the humans.

This dude is old. Really old. Even older than your grandpa! (Yep, we know, amazing!) He was plying his demonic trade earlier than 1000 BC.

In ancient Mesopotamia (modern-day Iraq, plus bits of Syria and Turkey), Pazuzu is referred to directly in the ancient scrolls and tablets of both the Assyrians (Big Men on Campus from late 2500 or early 2400–608 BC) and the Babylonians.

The famous Assyrian tablets were clay tablets inscribed with cuneiform script, a type of ancient writing from the Middle East. The king's royal scribes would jot down daily

47

happenings on the tablets—even the most ridiculous nonsense, such as whose turn it was to clean out the cesspit and how to read a sheep's liver to divine the future. Kind of like an ancient equivalent of a blog!

When on your monster-hunting travels, be sure to pop into France's *Musée du Louvre* (the Louvre Museum to you and us!) where you will find on display an impressive bronze figurine of Pazuzu cast in 700 BC.

Inscribed on the back of the statuette are the words "*I am Pazuzu, son of Hanpa, king of the evil spirits of the air which issues violently from mountains, causing much havoc.*"

(Check out the Louvre's ultra-cool official audio guide mobile app to learn more about the Pazuzu statue and hundreds of other fascinating historical objects!)

And then hitch a ferry ride to Britain across the always-chilly English Channel to eyeball what may possibly be an even older bronze amulet head of Pazuzu in London's British Museum, crafted between 800–500 B.C.

There are even Pazuzu head pendants to be seen at the Metropolitan Museum of Art in New York City, circa 800–700 BC! Paz was smart enough to license out the rights to his image and has made a killing through merchandising!

FYI: Most people think Beatrix Potter's Peter Rabbit was the world's first licensed character—*The Tale of Peter Rabbit* was published in 1902 and the book sold 28,000 copies in the first year; a year later, the character had become a hugely popular soft toy— but nope, Paz beat little Pete by a couple of thousand years!

The most ruthless and destructive of all the underworld's demon-gods, Pazuzu is described as having an almost fleshless canine or lion's head with a death-mask grimace. His body is that of an emaciated adult male human covered in scales, with two pairs of wings. Deadly hand talons, clawed eagle's feet, and a scorpion's tail finish off his rakish appearance.

Utterly devoid of compassion or mercy, this frightening desert scavenger rides the Arabian southwest winds, sowing storms, pestilence, plague, drought, and famine with his dry, fiery breath!

If you do manage to track him down, there is one sure way to protect yourself from Pazuzu's terrible wrath. You must stand facing the demon while loudly incanting a magical spell. This necromantic formula is sixteen lines long, so no, we're not going to repeat it here!

CASE STUDY 907/92P

Professor Emeritus in Assyriology (clever clog who studies ancient Assyrian history) from the University of Copenhagen, Mr. Ey Reed Gobbledygook, is one of many scholars worldwide currently translating cuneiform text from the Assyrian tablets into modern language.

The professor has kindly given us permission to publish some of his latest translations, which concern the demon Pazuzu!

The following text records an event in the forests outside the Assyrian royal city of Nimrud (ancient Kalhu) in 670 BC. Esarhaddon, king of the Assyrians (who reigned from 681–669 BC), was out hunting with his retinue of servants when they were confronted by the demon Pazuzu. —Professor E. R. G.

TABLET I63

Line

47 The horse of our lord reared up in great fear

48 There was much panic and terror among his men.

49 The king did speak most bravely.

50 Come, demon, what ails you?

5I The face of Pazuzu scowled death.

52 I answer to no human, king, or lackey, man.

53 Pazuzu opened his mouth and breathed on the servants of our lord.

54 Black boils sprang up, covering their faces and hands. They fell screaming. All were dead.

55 The king spoke once more. I am Esarhaddon, king of all Assyrians. I have no terror of demons.

56 Our lord came unto Pazuzu. With sword he split his scalp.

57 He trod upon his hinder part.

58 He severed the arteries of his blood.

59 The king skillfully contrived the ways of the gods. He spoke forth an incantation.

60 The north wind did spring up mightily to carry away the wounded Pazuzu into hidden places.

6I The king proclaimed, "No demon can best a king. I shall reign for one hundred years."

HOW TO DEFEAT PAZUZU

You know we said that the sixteen-line spell was too long for you to use on an attacking Paz? Well, we've come up with an ingenious solution! Record the incantation onto your smartphone and when confronting the demon, play it back loud at quadruple speed! What's that? We haven't told you the spell yet? Tch! Silly us! It's . . . oh . . . We're all out of room! Hey ho.

PAZUZU FACT FILE

Location: Middle East countries
Appearance: Ghastly!
Strength: Can lay waste to an entire continent with a single breath, so, you know . . .
Weaknesses: Magical incantation
Powers: Possible shape-shifter, flight, controls weather patterns, causes plagues and desolation, herald of the coming apocalypse and the destruction of all human life. (Cheerful, isn't he?!)
Fear Factor: 0.1 (in a good mood); 95.4 (in a bad mood)

Death's smile stretches wide
Cherry blossom falls to red
Life's song departed

rokurokubi

One of the scariest Japanese *yokai* is the dreaded Rokurokubi!

Its usual appearance is that of a young and attractive woman. But beware! Although they look and act human during the day, at night they reveal their true ghastly form.

Commonly referred to as "long necks," these totally twisted demons possess the awesome ability to stretch their necks to impossible lengths, allowing the head to travel almost independent of its body.

Humans and most other mammals, including giraffes, have seven neck vertebrae, although in the giraffe they can be as long as ten inches! (Those seven blocks of bone plus the head means these gentle giants are carrying around six hundred pounds of weight on their shoulders! Yowsers!)

The Rokurokubi has a similar number of vertebrae, although each one can stretch twelve feet. Stretching their necks across an entire town or village, they peer into windows, spying on unwary humans.

Tricksters by nature, Roku can't resist the urge to frighten humans. And the more extreme Roku love to drink human blood and eat people! (Our kind of demons! *Booshakka!*)

The best way to recognize these monstrosities is to get up close and personal. In human form, they will have distinct, pale stretch marks on the neck.

Occasionally, a hungry Rokurokubi will spend a fruitless night in search of prey. Growing tired, she falls asleep, forgetting to retract her long neck. If she's discovered, terrified villagers fetch their sharpest axes and then—*shunnk!* Off with her head!

Once you've tracked and trapped your prey, follow the villagers' example and decapitate it—this needs to be done quickly, as they are extremely fast and agile—and then bury the body far away from the head. (Bury the head first; this way, it can't see where you've buried the body.)

A Rokurokubi takes hours to die and during this time can still reattach its head to its body. So if you don't want to be on the receiving end of bloody revenge, stand guard over the burial ground until you're absolutely sure it's dead!

For many hundreds—if not thousands!—of years, there was a tradition in Japan where family and friends would gather in the room of a house at night and light exactly one hundred candles.

With shadows flickering all around them, they began to tell bloodcurdling true stories from Japanese folklore and legends.

At the end of each story, one of the candles would be extinguished. The room would slowly shrink into the darkness, the stories themselves growing ever more terrifying.

With the final story told and the final candle extinguished, the room would be plunged into pure night!

Everyone sat quietly in the dark, listening to the chatter of invisible spirits and demons swirling all around them!

We recently unearthed one of these stories on a scroll at the burial site of an unknown peasant.

The Demon and the Cherry Blossom Tree

Many centuries ago, there grew in the center of the small village of Tsui the most magnificent sakura (cherry blossom) tree. Its beauty was admired by all who laid eyes upon it.

Yet in all its years of growth, and throughout all of the seasons, its flowers never fell from its branches.

One day, the new mayor of the town decided that the tree blocked the light through the window of his home.

"This tree is a nuisance. It must be removed," commanded he. "On the morrow, the woodman must cut it down."

The people of the village were greatly upset. "The tree does nothing, yet gives much pleasure," said a wise old man.

The mayor stood steadfast in his decision. "That tree must go!" he said.

That night, in the home of a beautiful young woman new to the village, a strange transformation took place. Looking out into the darkness and seeing no one around, she began to stretch her neck.

"I hunger," hissed the demon entity Rokurokubi, stretching her neck all around the village, looking for prey to feast upon. "I need human blood."

She espied the mayor returning unsteadily from a night of merriment. He stood under the sakura tree to catch his breath.

"Foolish man!" snarled the Rokurokubi, flicking her neck sharply forward. "You are mine!"

53

Alarmed, the terrified mayor could not move. The demon opened its mouth to reveal sharp fangs, dripping saliva, ready to sink into his flabby throat.

And then, as if weeping for the death of a human, the flowers of the sakura tree began to fall.

At first in ones and twos, and then in a continuous light shower of soft white petals on the black night.

They looked so beautiful that the Rokurokubi stopped, transfixed. In that instant the woodcutter, returning from the forest and seeing what was occurring, swung his ax and cleaved the Rokurokubi's head from its neck.

The mayor now understood that the sakura tree was the sacred heart of the village. Instead of removing the tree, he moved his home, but only so far as to be able to look upon the cherry blossom tree every morning when he awoke.

ROKUROKUBI FACT FILE

Location: Japan
Appearance: Stretchy-necked woman
Strength: Can reattach its head
Weaknesses: Can't resist snooping!
Powers: The ability to stretch its head to the local 7-Eleven to pick up a carton of milk without leaving home. (Also, neat shape-shifting/neck-stretching combo.)
Fear Factor: 42.7

HOW TO CATCH A ROKUROKUBI

Hve yue evr hd onne ov thooss dais whr noe maturr hhowwe hurd yoo tri, uu keyp maykin silee spallin mersticks?

Well, the next time your English teacher gives you an F for your course work you can say, "Hey, teach, t'werent me, t'was Titivillus, the scrag!" (Unless you really are that bad at spelling, in which case you need help—fast!)

Strongly suspected of being behind the creation of texts and tweets, where spelling, punctuation, and grammatical errors are supposedly "cool" (sad, we know), the invisible demon Titivillus has been tricking humans into misspelling since at least ancient Babylonian times.

An independent state from 1894–539 BC, Babylon was already a religious and cultural center when the Akkadian emperor Sargon ruled the roost from 2334–2279 BC.

The Babylonians were passionate readers—there were libraries in almost every town and temple—and Titivillus delighted in messing up the latest best-seller clay tablets with endless orthography snafus!

Titi later popped up in the fourth century AD, in the monasteries of Egyptian ascetics (religious dudes who deprive themselves of any material pleasures in the hope of spiritual advancement; hey, whatever rocks your boat!), where he went from being the demon of calligraphy to the recording

ALL THESE SOCIAL NETWORKING SITES REALLY MAKE IT EASY TO SPREAD LIES, GOSSIP, AND SPELLING MISTAKES.

DON'T CHA JUST LOVE TECHNOLOGY? HEE-HEE-HEE-HEE-HEEEEE!

demon (and busybody), conscientiously jotting down all the various sins that the monks and townsfolk admitted committing.

He then stuffed the sins into his big sack and took them back to his boss, Satan, who used them against departing souls on the Day of Judgment!

Nine centuries later and 2,230 miles away, in the leafy lanes of old England (not forgetting the rest of the UK), Titivillus is heard creeping about in church rafters, collecting the idle chat of gossiping churchgoers, and noting mumbled or skipped words in hymns and prayers.

In his chart-topping smash blockbuster *Tractatus de Penitentia* (circa 1285), Johannes Galensis, John of Wales, makes the first reference to Titivillus in the Latin language:

Fragmina verborum
Titivillus colligit horum
Quibus die mille
Vicibus se sarcinat ille.

Which roughly translates from the Latin as: *Titivillus packs his bag with verbal detritus a thousand times a day!*

The so-called Renaissance era, which started in Italy in the 1300s and spread across Europe in the late 1400s (ending around 1600), saw a sharp increase in the education of the masses, and an unstoppable tsunami of intellectual curiosity and artistic creativity began.

The movement received a much-needed kick-start in 1440, when a German blacksmith, goldsmith, printer, and publisher named Johannes Gutenberg invented the world's first movable-type printing press (circa the early fifteenth century).

With mass-market printing followed a veritable explosion of reading materials, from leaflets and pamphlets to newspapers, magazines, and books. And Titivillus was there to make sure the *typo* (typographical error) was born!

Guess what? Titivillus is with us still, gaily messing up millions of Internet sites with badly mangled grammar and spelling, omissions, inaccuracies, and downright lies.

He's in his element, filling his sack daily with the moronic Internet chat, gossip, and slander that fills the World Wide Web.

Satan's servant now has many more souls to offer his master!

CASE STUDY 113/86T

Aside from messing with your school assignments and sneaking major typos into best-selling books, Titivillus writes a weekly gossip column for Purgatory's Brimstone Enquirer, digging the dirt on Satan's hellish hordes.

And at no little danger to ourselves, we've managed to get our hands on one of Titivillus's latest columns! Read on, Macduff!

DEMONS ARE FATTIES—FACT!

There are billions of disgusting humans infecting the planet. They guzzle down saturated fat-filled junk food like there's no tomorrow. (And the way they carry on, there won't be!)

Much of the developed world's population is overweight, and they're getting more obese by the year! And the next generation is going to be even bigger! Wowsers!

This is great for us li'l devils, because all that corpulent blubber carries with it a much higher risk of clogged veins and major heart disease! Woo-hoo!

And when those humans suffer a massive cardiac arrest at an early age, with their heart swelling up and going KAAA-BLOOEY, we'll be there to drag their corrupted souls down to the fiery pits of Hell! That'll help them lose weight!

But, hey, don't crow yet, fellow demons, because some of us are piling on the pounds, too! Have you caught sight of Batibat lately? Wooo-eeeee! She's a dumpling if ever there was one! And those Jinn could do with losing a few pounds!

The latest report by the HMA (Hades Medical Association) notes that 56 percent of the Underworld's denizens are either overweight (23 percent) or massively obese (33 percent)!

So I guess it's time to cut down on fat-soaked human flesh (tasty though it is!) and start adding more fruit and fiber to our meals!

WHAT TO DO WITH TITIVILLUS

Bribe Titi to mess up the dates on calendars so that your mom thinks there's a week of vacation from school——*every other week!*

TITIVILLUS FACT FILE

Location: The world
Appearance: Demon-y. (How should we know?! He's invisible!!)
Strength: Since "the pen is mightier than the sword" (the adage first coined by English author Edward Bulwer-Lytton for his play *Richelieu; or, The Conspiracy in 1839*), then we guess kind of unimaginably powerful!
Weaknesses: A good dictionary or spell-checker should do the trick!
Powers: Invisibility. Typographical errors and strangled grammar.
Fear Factor: 6

YAN-GANT-Y-TAN

There are some serious demons out there in Ghoulsville, and another to add to the list of supernatural bugly (butt ugly) creepoids to hunt down is the nighttime French terror with the all-singing, all-dancing moniker of Yan-gant-y-tan!

Yan, as we prefer to call him (for obvious reasons), wanders the quiet country roads of Finistère in Brittany (a cultural region in the northwest of the country), scaring the bejeebers out of good honest folk.

(Travel note: The Latin name for Finistère is *Finis Terræ*, meaning "end of the earth." Its name in the Breton language is *Penn ar Bed,* meaning "head/end of the world." Basically, it's the westernmost part of France—you can't travel farther than Finistère without falling headfirst into the Atlantic Ocean!)

French occultist (someone interested in the paranormal and supernatural), demonologist, and writer Collin de Plancy (Jacques Albin Simon Collin de Plancy to give the guy his full handle; he was born in 1793 or 1794, and died sometime around 1861) penned a book in 1818 that he titled *Dictionnaire Infernal*, covering all then-current knowledge of demonology.

Well, by the time someone revised the book in 1863—the most famous and successful of all the editions due to de Plancy adding sixty-nine illustrations of hell-born demons to the pages—he had "found God," became Catholic, and was noticing demons popping out of every dark nook and cranny!

And one of Lucifer's legions featured in the *Dictionnaire Infernal* was that candle-loving freak better known as Yan-gant-y-tan!

What's so freaky about liking candles, you ask? Nothing, except that this demon likes to balance a long, lit candle on each of the fingers of his right hand. Twisted!

Described by his victims as either a hairy, wild man or possibly even troll-like in appearance, Yan waits down dark lanes or in the woods and forests until some poor, unsuspecting soul comes strolling past. Then he leaps out, caterwauling like a banshee, spinning his candles around like a flaming wheel! *Wooo-oooo-oooo!*

Anyone who falls foul of this fetid fiend can expect misery and misfortune to fall upon them, for a meeting with Yan is an omen of seriously bad things to come!

Other times, Yan may be feeling more sweet-natured. If you happen along at night and your lantern or torch gives out, Yan'll pop out of the bushes and present you with five of your own lit candles to help you on your way!

CASE STUDY 557/8YGT

So where does Yan get all those candles for his fingers? Well, demons don't usually have much loose change jangling around in their pockets—heck, most don't even have pockets!

So Yan is something of a B&E (breaking and entering) specialist. His favorite places to raid are, naturally, candle factories!

(FYI: Some genius Chinese dude made the world's first candles from whale blubber around 200 BC.)

YAN-GANT-Y-TAN CANDLES

Finistère
Soap & Candle Works

Here's a report by a security guard at a candle factory, regarding a recent attempted break-in. (Translated from le français, naturellement!)

Finistère Soap & Candle Company
Rue du Cuisses de Grenouilles
Fouesnant
Finistère

Incident Report

Report Date/time: June 17/2:40 a.m.

Point of Contact (POC) Information

Name: Jean Logis-Porche
Title: Security Guard

Summary

A break-in of the factory occurred during the early morning of June 17. The perpetrator broke in through the skylight and was confronted by the security guard, who attempted to apprehend him.

Details of the Incident

I was making my rounds, as usual, at two forty precisely, when I heard a noise coming from the east wing. I could see lights flickering in the dimness. "Zut alors!" I gasped. "Feu!"

Hurrying over, I expected to find a small fire caused by an electrical fault. (Such events have occurred before.)

Instead, I encountered what can only be described as a grotesque and naked man-creature, his entire body covered in thick hair.

At his feet were a few wooden crates that had once contained a shipment of candles. The crates had been violently smashed open, their contents scattered about.

The creature addressed me, growling softly, and held out his right hand. To my bewilderment, I saw that the creature was balancing lit candles on each of his fingers and thumb. He began to spin his hand around slowly in front of me.

Deducing that he was a madman who had escaped from a lunatic asylum, I withdrew my revolver and ordered him to "j'arrête!"

The creature glanced at the remaining crates stacked up all around us. Then I heard a loud creaking sound. Looking up, I saw the crates toppling toward me.

When I regained consciousness, the creature was gone. It was just bad luck that the crates had chosen that moment to fall; otherwise, I would have apprehended the perpetrator.

Name: M. J. Logis-Porche

Title: Head of Security

HOW TO DEFEAT YAN-GANT-Y-TAN

Take a deep breath, and——BLOW!!

YAN-GANT-Y-TAN FACT FILE

Location: Finistère, France
Appearance: Hairy dude or troll (no, not the kind you find on the Internet!)
Strength: Puny for a demon, strong for a human
Weaknesses: Yan has to move very slowly in case his candles extinguish! If he zaps you with badness, leave a small bag of gold around a road marker. Yan will steal it and leave you alone for another night!
Powers: Bad luck hex. Candle power! (Oooh! Save us!)
Fear Factor: 83.3

Location: The Sakha (Yakutia) Republic in the Russian Federation

Appearance: One-eyed, one-armed, one-legged demons riding two-headed, eight-legged, two-tailed dragons. Their leader, *Alyp Khara Aat Mogoidoon*, is a giant who has three heads, six arms, six legs, and a body made of iron!

Strength: How strong can a one-armed demon be?!

Weaknesses: If you're frightened of a one-of-everything demon, then frankly, you're an embarrassment! (Their leader is another matter, of course . . . he's terrifying!!)

Powers: The power to make monster hunters burst out laughing at their appearance. Also, they kind of eat people—if they can ever catch any, that is!

Fear Factor: 2.5 (and we're being generous)

ABBASY

Location: The island of Bali, Indonesia

Appearance: Monstrous size, bulging eyes, huge belly, and missing or exaggerated body parts.

Strength: Prodigious

Weaknesses: The Ogoh-ogoh Carnival on Nyepi Day (the Day of Silence—the Balinese New Year's Day), when all demons and monsters are exorcised from the villages so that the Balinese can start the new year afresh. (The Day of Silence is like the radical opposite of our Western New Year celebrations. The name means just that— all sound is banished for the whole day! No traffic (neither vehicles nor people—you have to stay inside your home; the streets must remain completely empty), no work, no entertainment (yep, no computers, TV, radio, or music!), and talking only in whispers, if at all. Total, utter silence! Then, at night, it's Ogoh-Ogoh—party time!

Powers: The Buta Kala are to blame for everything! War, pestilence, strife, earthquakes, volcanic eruptions, floods, asteroids crashing to Earth, arguments, sadness, greed, politicians, your mom burning dinner, your dad crashing the car, your little sibling driving you nuts! It's all the fault of Buta Kala! So mondo powerful then!

Fear Factor: 89.4

BUTA KALA

ELOKO

Location: Rainforests of the Democratic Republic of the Congo, Africa (the Congo River is the deepest river in the world, at a depth of 720 feet)

Appearance: Hairless, but with a face and body that are covered in a thick coat of grass. The Eloko have long, sharp claws; eyes of fire; large snouts; and a mouth that can extend to swallow an adult human in one gulp!

Strength: Compared to other demons, kind of puny . . .

Weaknesses: Can be killed in similar ways to any human: arrows, bullets, beheading, a rock to the noggin, watching daytime TV . . . also susceptible to amulets and fetishes (a man-made object of supernatural power)

Powers: Possess tiny magical bells, which they ring to bewitch their prey before eating them

Fear Factor: 27.3

GORGONS

Location: Mediterranean and the underworld (of which they are queens)

Appearance: Hair of living snakes (cool!); large, staring eyes; sharp tusks or fangs; lolling tongue; scaly body; hands made of brass; leathery wings; and a beard. (Um, yeah, we didn't want to bring up your facial-hair problems, ladies, but . . . gross!)

Strength: Godlike, on account of they steal power from the gods. Can kill anyone who stands in their way. (So, an attack from behind may be in order. Cowardly, we know, but hey . . .)

Weaknesses: Beheading usually does the trick

Powers: One glance at their hideous faces will turn you to stone! Hellfire from their hands will incinerate you! Flight. Command of the storms and the seas. Can create famines and pestilence. Shape-shifters; can disguise themselves as human. Blood taken from the left side of a Gorgon can bring the dead back to life. Blood taken from the right side will kill instantly!

Fear Factor: 97.6

IKWAOKINYAPIPPILELE

Location: Panama, Central America, and Colombia, South America
Appearance: It's a shape-shifter, take your pick!
Strength: Well, it fights off other demons single-handedly, so you've got to be impressed . . .
Weaknesses: A strong headache remedy should do the trick. (See below.)
Powers: Nocturnal demon of the Kuna people (of which there are only fifty thousand left in the world). Not so much evil as a downright pest. He guards the night, preying on other demons that spread disease. However, Ikwaokinyapippilele also has a neat selection of headaches on tap for anyone who annoys him, from your basic eyestrain to a brain tumor. He'll also throw spears at heroes during battle, just for the fun of it. Can disguise himself as the three bright stars in a row in the constellation Orion (aka Orion's Sword).
Fear Factor: 3.8

KISHI

Location: Angola, southern Africa
Appearance: Two-faced; has a handsome man's face on the front of its head and a hyena's face on the back that is hidden by long, thick hair
Strength: Long, sharp teeth and extra-powerful jaws. Once it bites you, there is no escape!
Weaknesses: Offer to wash its hair, and then squirt shampoo in its face! Man, does that sting!
Powers: Smooth-talking and charming, it chats up young women and invites them home for a candlelit dinner—then it eats them with its hyena face!
Fear Factor: 52

NYBBAS

Location: Your dreams
Appearance: A terrifying, smiling face. No one has ever seen his eyes, which are always hidden, either behind a veil or a hat.
Strength: Puny. Only attacks victims in their sleep. Considered a fool and a swindler.
Weaknesses: Kindness, gentleness, generosity, and love weaken him to such an extent that he can be easily dispatched back to the underworld!
Powers: Manipulative. Disdainful. A liar. (Basically, like every politician we can name!) Causes nightmares and disturbed sleep. Whispers insidious thoughts to sleeping people, which they will then act out when awake. Nybbas is believed to be behind the invention of television and the World Wide Web, which he controls alongside radio, magazines, and especially newspapers. He is trying to desensitize and dehumanize humans, encouraging selfishness and cruelty. In this manner, he hopes to destroy the human race. (And by the current state of the world, his nefarious plan seems to be working!)
Fear Factor: 88.8

ONI

Location: Japan
Appearance: Wickedly evil. Giant-size with wildly long hair, cat-like fangs, razor-sharp claws, and two demon horns sprouting from its head! Some Oni have extra eyes, fingers, and toes for added scariness. Their skin can be any color, but many prefer a putrid shade of red or blue.
Strength: Invincible. Unbeatable . . .
Weaknesses: . . . except for . . . holly! And monkey statues! And buildings facing northeast! (Sheesh!) And . . . jeez, this is embarrassing . . . soy beans! Every year on February 3, the day before the start of spring (Risshun), the Japanese participate in Setsubun (aka Bean-Throwing Festival or Bean-Throwing Ceremony). The special ritual is called mamemaki (literally "bean-throwing"), which chases away all evil spirits and demons, such as Oni.

Powers: Invisibility. Flight. Can cause disasters, spread death-dealing diseases, control the weather, hocus-pocus you with bad luck, turn milk sour, let the air out of your bike tires, make you forget to do your homework—you know, total evilness like that . . .
Fear Factor: 32.1 (admittedly, they look scary, but . . . y'know . . . soy beans! Wowsers!)

PUKWUDGIES

Location: Forests of Massachusetts, United States
Appearance: (Don't laugh!) Two to three feet tall; large nose, ears, and fingers; gray skin that glows
Strength: They may look puny, but they have magic on their side!
Weaknesses: Hmm, we'll get back to you on that . . .
Powers: Magic. Shape-shifters who can transform into animals. Able to appear and disappear in an instant. Can create fire (and set victims alight) at will. Skilled archers who attack with magical arrows dripping with deadly poison. Souls of the victims (usually from the Wampanoag Nation) are balls of light known as *Tei-Pai-Wankas*. The Pukwudgies use these soul-balls to attract other natives into the forests so they may kidnap or kill them and steal their souls. They also get a kick out of kidnapping children and burning villages.
Fear Factor: 46

QANDISA

Location: Rivers and streams of Morocco, north Africa
Appearance: Usually a beautiful young woman with bright green or blue hair made from smoke
Strength: Magical
Weaknesses: Human or animal sacrifice, or other offerings. When in smoky mist form, a giant fan may blow her apart. In solid form, good old decapitation should do the trick!
Powers: A female jinn, Qandisa possesses uber-powerful magic. Shape-shifter. Flight. Hypnotism. She lures young men into the water and they are never seen again.
Fear Factor: 31.9

T'AO-T'IEH

Location: China (T'ao-T'ieh may have existed as far back as the neolithic Liangzhu culture (aka jade culture) of 3400-2250 BC, and were definitely sighted during the Shang Dynasty (approximately 1600-1050 BC).

Appearance: Mugly flesh-eating critters with huge head and legs, but no body! Their oversize mouths take up most of the face, but they have no lower jaw. From a curled upper lip protrudes huge fangs and dagger-size teeth. Can shape-shift into a tiger or human with two stomachs.

Strength: Mega!

Weaknesses: With no body, anything it eats comes out safely on the other side of its mouth!

Powers: Its name means glutton for the simple fact that it can swallow an adult human whole!

Fear Factor: 3.7 (scary but not deadly, for a highly trained monster hunter)

ZAR

Location: Ethiopia, country in the Horn of Africa (second most populous country in Africa with more than 84 million people. Believed to be the country where *Homo sapiens* first left Africa to spread out across the world between 60,000 and 125,000 years ago.)

Appearance: Demon with a leopard's head

Strength: Powerful enough to destroy other demons. (Some victims allow Zar to possess them to destroy other demons that are threatening them. Wow! Definitely an "out of the frying pan and into the fire" scenario to us!)

Weaknesses: Exorcism, or a possessed body being whipped. This will make Zar leave the body.

Powers: Mind control and body possession, but only of unmarried women. The possessed woman stares blankly into space, growling, snarling, and writhing like a leopard!

Fear Factor: 51

ELEMENTALS

In olde dayes of the king Arthour
(In olden days of King Arthur)

Al was this lond fulfilled of fayrie
(All of this land was filled with fairies)

—*Geoffrey Chaucer—philosopher, alchemist, astronomer,*
author (circa 1343–1400)

Okay, fingers on buzzers! For an extra ten points in our freaky fantabulous *Monster Hunt* pop quiz: "What is an elemental?"

If any of you shout out, "Which one? There are currently 118 listed on the periodic table!" out the window you go!

We're not talking about the elements! (Which, FYI, are substances like carbon, oxygen, arsenic, silicon, gold, copper, zinc, lead, etc., that are made up entirely from one type of atom!)

There are four basic elements of nature: air, fire, earth, and water. (The ancient Greeks reckoned there were actually five elements, the other being a bizarre element that they called *aether*, which is supposedly the absolute essence—the "thing that it is"—of a substance, but we don't need to bother ourselves with such nonsense here!)

Within each of the four elements are nature *spirits*—elementals—which are living creatures that control and shape the elements from which they were born. These include everything from pixies, elves, leprechauns, giants, ogres, dragons, mermaids, trolls, gnomes, devas, tree and water sprites, fairies, and the like, and believe us, these aren't the cute, friendly characters you remember from fairy tales. They're utterly depraved, malicious, vicious, and insanely evil! (Yeah, we know—cool!)

Animism is the oldest known human spiritual practice (a "religion," if you like), and its followers believe that elementals inhabit *everything*! Yep, they're in plants, animals, rocks, concrete, bricks, trees, mud, slime, algae, elephant droppings, belly-button fluff, chewed-up bubble gum, blood, snot, puke—the whole caboodle! Everything LIVES! *Aaaaaaaaaaah!!*

This ancient faith is still practiced worldwide today, including by the Australian Aborigines, who have one of the oldest continuous cultures stretching back at least 170,000 years!

German-Swiss Renaissance physician, botanist, astrologer, alchemist, occultist, and all-around show-off Paracelsus (born Philippus Aureolus Theophrastus Bombastus von Hohenheim—yowsers! Painful! No wonder he changed his moniker!—and living from 1493–1541) was the first to group these elementals into four elements:

Sylph—Air Elemental

Salamander—Fire Elemental

Gnome—Earth Elemental

Undine or nymph—Water Elemental

It was ole Paracelsus, one of the most influential medical scientists of his time, who first established the role of chemistry in medicine. He is also acknowledged as giving zinc its name, originally labeling it *zincum* (symbol Zn, atomic number thirty, first element of group twelve of the periodic table), and for tagging three of the elementals: sylph, undine, and gnome.

Admittedly, there are some good and decent elementals out there (one such being the brownie, who loves to do the housework for humans), but we're hard-core monster hunters and it's the cruel, bloodthirsty, and murderous elementals that interest us! Yeah, baby!

Mostly invisible to humans, these creeps can be found in buildings, parks, rivers and swamps, woods and forests, up mountains, and under the sea! And they will strike without warning—or mercy!

And what do monster hunters do while the rest of lily-livered humanity is running around screaming in mortal terror? Sheesh! Whaddya think?! We strike back! Oh, yeah!

So, within the following pages are twenty-five of the world's most deadly and diabolical elementals for you to track down! (We know. We're too kind.)

And if you catch one, let us know. There's a good chance you'll appear in the prestigious Monster Hunters Hall of Fame!

Go get 'em, tiger!

Have you ever noticed that when you're cooped up in school facing a hideous day of math and science, the weather is always great? Yet on weekends, when it's your downtime, it's suddenly raining?

Some people consider this to be that strange paranormal phenomenon known as "just my luck." (This is not to be confused with the similar yet distinctly different experience of Murphy's Law, which is that if anything can go wrong, it will go wrong.)

However, although this strange occurrence does indeed have a supernatural bent, it has nothing to do with "luck" or "law," Murphy's or otherwise!

The true purveyor of these kooky, messed-up atmospheric conditions is none other than the hellish elemental spirit Ala!

An Ala (aka Hala, plural Ale or Hali) is one of the most powerful and deadly of all elementals. These ladies are so hardcore they periodically try to eat the moon *and* the sun. (Righteous!)

Although preferring to hang out around the open countryside of Bulgaria, Macedonia, and Serbia, their foul-weather conjurations are felt across the planet. These fetid ladies get their kicks by leading hail-producing thunderclouds over fields, orchards, and vineyards to destroy the freshly grown crops.

Malignant shape-shifters, Ale can grow to giant-size, gleefully ripping up trees and smashing houses into kindling.

They also spread rabies, which can infect a variety of animals. If a human is bitten by a rabid creature and the wound is not immediately treated, the virus will infect the central nervous system, causing a disease in the brain and a most agonizing death!

(Medical note: Before 1885, all cases of rabies were fatal. Then genius French chemist and microbiologist (someone who investigates microscopic organisms such as bacteria, algae, and fungi) Louis Pasteur (1822–1895) and his equally genius colleague Pierre Paul Émile Roux (1853–1933), a physician, bacteriologist, and immunologist (an investigator of the immune system of organisms), created a vaccine. Unfortunately, around 55,000 people still die of the disease every year. So before hunting Ale, make sure your rabies shots are up-to-date!)

Ale have voracious appetites. They will eat everything in their path, and their favorite snack to chow down on is kids!

Oh, and if all that wasn't enough, Ale can shape-shift into whatever they fancy, possess the bodies of men, and, if feeling really nasty, turn a human blind, deaf, or lame, or drive them insane!

CASE STUDY 475/41A

Even demons and monsters deserve a little downtime from terrorizing humans. Their favorite way to chill out is by watching hell's number one television channel, Purgatory TV.

Among all the bloodletting cooking shows and gore-fest reality programs, hourly meteorological forecasts are presented by, naturally, an Ala!

"Take it away, Susan!"

"Well, for those of you who went out today, I don't have to tell you that conditions were delightfully atrocious across the planet. I'm pleased to say that a 17,000-feet-high dust devil smashed a path of total devastation through southwest Australia, from Perth to Albany, sucking up tens of thousands of humans before spitting them out again.

"If you're in the area, take a helicopter ride and check out all the impressive blood splatters that can now be seen.

"Iran in the Middle East is always kind of dry, so we kindly deposited one hundred tons of rainwater on the country, which is now the world's largest fishing lake.

"Demons who like chomping on putrefying human flesh—grab your rod and start reeling them in!

"Heavy snow has resulted in the whole of Europe being frozen in a solid block of ice; anyone living there won't see a thaw for at least six months, but hey—they're all stiffs now, so they won't care.

HUMPH! SUNSHINE AND CLEAR SKIES SHE SAID...
GURR! NEVER TRUST AN ALA WEATHER FORECAST
...GRUMBLE...GRUMBLE...

OR, FOR THAT MATTER, A HUMAN ONE!

"There are giant tsunamis pounding the continent of Africa, solar flares vaporizing Australia, howling blizzards in Asia, and for our favorite continent, North America, everything, all at once!

"And that's all for today's weather!"

WHAT TO DO WITH AN ALA

Build a wind turbine in your backyard and offer an Ala one of your siblings for lunch in return for her creating a small, never-ending whirlwind around the machine.

ALA FACT FILE

Location: In the clouds, lakes, springs, caves, mountains, forests, or gigantic trees in Bulgaria, Macedonia, and Serbia

Appearance: A shape-shifter, so basically anything. They have a fondness for appearing as a black cloud; black, drill-shaped whirlwind; dark fog; a giant creature of indefinite form; a raven; a female dragon; a huge-mouthed human or snakelike monster with three heads, six wings, and twelve tails, or a horse's head and serpent's body; or perhaps a bull with huge horns.

Strength: Some elementals claim to be able to eat the sun! The SUN!!

Weaknesses: Your pet dragon is a good bet (what do you mean, you don't have one?! Sheesh!), or failing that, an eagle. (Oh, come on. You must have one of them!) Take a religious saint along on your hunt, or better yet a zmajeviti (a man born of human mother and dragon father), both of whom have enough godlike powers to zap the elemental. Otherwise, confront the Ala alone, shouting out this powerful magical spell: "Alo, ne ovamo, putuj na Tatar planinu!" ("Ala, not hither, travel to the Tartar Mountain!") Works for us!

Powers: Invisibility, shape-shifting, flying, weather control, disease carrier

Fear Factor: 98.3

WEEKLY EXAMINER

EW! STRANGE UNEXPECTED BIZARRE and all TRUE

THE WORLD'S MOST RELIABLE NEWSPAPER

BATHHOUSE BEAST!

EXCLUSIVE REPORT BY NEELA NIGHTSHADE

We're not ones to poke fun at another person's customs or traditions, but you've got to admit, there are some really kooky ones out there.

For instance, in Russia and the Ukraine, many people, even today, celebrate their most important life events, including birth, marriage, and even death . . . in the bath!

After a funeral, the mourners of the dear departed meet up at a *bania*—aka *banya*, a public bathhouse—and all climb naked into a large steam bath together so that their beloved will be warm for that long journey to the afterlife.

Banias have been around for thousands of years. In the early first century, Jesus's disciples Andrew (later Saint Andrew) and his bro Simon Peter (Saint Peter) visited a *bania* on their travels to the territories that later became Russia and Ukraine.

He wrote in his journal: *"They warm them to extreme heat, then undress, and after anointing themselves with tallow* (beef or mutton fat—ewww!), *take young reeds and lash their bodies . . . They actually lash themselves so violently that they barely escape alive. Then they drench themselves in cold water and are thus revived."*

(We'll give that a miss, thanks!)

And behind the red-hot stoves or under the benches of *banias* lurks that loathsome elemental, the Bannik, waiting to strike!

The Bannik is described as a short, crinkly humanoid with hairy paws and long fingernails.

Appearing only if the bath is dirty or someone is disrespectful—to talk, boast, lie, sing, or swear is a major no-no—the Bannik will fly into a terrible rage. Attacking his intended victims with red-hot coals or boiling water, this vicious elemental flays off their skin and wraps the bodies around a steaming hot stove!

The Bannik expects humans to keep a clean, well-heated bath, otherwise he can transform harmless steam into deadly coal gas to suffocate you!

Protection from a Bannik attack includes making the sign of the cross before entering, wishing other bathers a good bath, and when leaving, loudly wishing the Bannik a hearty goodbye.

A monster hunter needs smarts to catch sight of a Bannik. It's best to go alone, strip down to your bathing suit, and step your right foot into a bath's steaming water. Take your cross from around your neck and place it under the heel of your left foot. The Bannik may then appear!

Neela Nightshade, ace reporter for the Weekly
World Examiner, recently filed this report.

BATTHOUSE BEAST!

Weekly World Examiner Exclusive

OYMYAKON, RUSSIA—January 5

Russia has the coldest inhabited places on Earth.

The coldest? Oymyakon, a village of between five hundred and eight hundred people (depending on whom you ask), which has an average winter chill factor of -58°F/-50°C! In really "cold years," this place records temperatures in the low -90s°F/-68°C. Yet schools only close when the temperature drops to a senses-numbing -52°F/-46°C!

I'm here to investigate reports of that brutal elemental spirit, the Bannik, attacking bathers in the local bathhouse.

Outside, the dense, freezing fog tears at your lungs. Your eyes can't water because your tear ducts are frozen.

Inside the *bania*, my view is curtailed by a thick curtain of fiery steam. I'm sweltering under triple layers of winter clothes, but there are some things I draw the line at, and going au naturel to grab an exclusive is one of them!

Hesitantly, I step toward the tiled bath.

The Bannik's recent handiwork is on display. Strips of bloodied human flesh are exhibited on the floor like bacon strips on a delicatessen counter. Gross!

This reporter has not come to threaten the Bannik, merely to consult him. The Bannik is known to tell a young woman's fortune during the yuletide season.

Kneeling, I humbly make the sign of the cross and present my offerings:

luxurious bath salts, lye (caustic soda), and birch twigs.

I wait. The silence is oppressive. Suddenly, there is the sound of small, wet feet slapping in steam puddles behind me.

I immediately sense who it is. His spiritual aura is overwhelming.

Hairy hands reach out and pick up the gifts. Childish giggling echoes around the chamber. The Bannik is pleased by my offerings.

Your future is told by the Bannik touching you from behind. A warm touch means much happiness awaits, a cold touch is a dire warning of ill fortune.

I swallow hard; my fate is literally in his hands.

Long, sharp talons run gently down my exposed neck . . . and my body violently arcs as a paroxysm of glacial agony tears through!

Gasping, my body topples forward. Through the pain, I hear a quiet splash in the water. Unable to clearly think, my hand works on its own accord, snapping a shot on my cell phone, capturing the moment for all eternity.

I have my exclusive . . .

. . . but it appears that my future . . . looks grim.

HOW TO KILL A BANNIK

Wait for winter and then open the door to the *bania* to let out the steam. The Bannik will literally *freeze* to death!

BANNIK FACT FILE

Location: Russia, Ukraine
Appearance: Wizened old guy suffering from hypertrichosis (an abnormal amount of hair) on his hands, and in need of a large nail file
Strength: Average for an elemental
Weaknesses: Not so much a weakness, but if you want to placate the Bannik, choke a black chicken and bury the body under the building site of a new bania. When the bathhouse is officially open, throw salt over the stove of the first heating. You'll be good buds forevermore.
Powers: The power to make humans clean the bath properly behind them
Fear Factor: 46

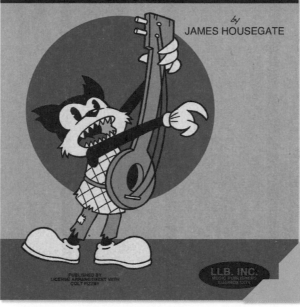

THREE CHEERS
FOR BOGIE!

by
JAMES HOUSEGATE

PUBLISHED BY
LICENSE ARRANGEMENT WITH
COLT FIZZBY

L.L.B., INC.
MUSIC PUBLISHERS
ERADMOX CITY

The very best localities worldwide to track down elemental and faerie folk are the four countries that make up the United Kingdom: England, Wales, Scotland, and Northern Ireland.

FYI: The Republic of Ireland, although sharing the same landmass as Northern Ireland, is considered a separate sovereign state following a bloody civil war of independence. The war began in January 1919 and ended in July 1921 at the cost of more than 3,400 lives. The republic came into being the following year.

The UK is where you'll find a veritable cornucopia of faeries, elves, gnomes, pixies, goblins, hobgoblins, dwarfs, trolls, sprites, knockers, brownies, bogles, bugbears, spriggans, changelings, pooka, mermaids, dragons, will-o'-the-wisp, ogres, giants, and all mad combinations thereof! (And this isn't even counting the kazillions of ghosts and the crazy paranormal activities that go on there!)

One can hardly walk down the street without tripping over fey, and the very air itself tingles with an electrical discharge of vast supernatural origins. The UK is a monster hunter's treasure trove of unearthly delights!

"Oop North," as people in the South playfully refer to the North of England (due in part to the northern accent), has many a demonic spirit lurking in the hills and dales, villages and towns.

One such is the malevolent Boggart, a mischief-maker, child abductor, murderer, and flesh-eater who delights in making human lives a misery!

Boggarts are frequently peeped hanging out in the counties of Lancashire and Yorkshire.

(Travel note: Yorkshire is the largest county (district) in the UK and has been inhabited since the last Ice Age, around 8000 BC. The area was first referred to by name in the *Anglo-Saxon Chronicle* in 1065. The *Chronicle* was a manuscript that recorded events chronologically, year by year. The first of these appeared in the late ninth century during the reign of King Alfred the Great, who lived from 849–899.)

Boggarts take many forms, including a squat, ugly, hairy humanoid with bestial attributes, and with or without arms the length of fishing rods. Or a type of *satyr*, a half-man, half-goat creature. Then again, perhaps it's the size of a calf, with long, shaggy hair and eyes like saucers!

There are boggarts who prefer home comforts and those who enjoy the wild outdoors. Home boggarts are annoying pests who hide things, rearrange furniture, break pots, turn the milk sour, injure dogs, and even—gasp!—pull the blankets off your bed on cold winter nights! (Oooh! The beasts!) They are also the cause of Things That Go Bump in the Night!

Warning: Never give your home boggart a name; otherwise, he will stay with your family for life! Even if you move homes to escape his destructive rampages, the boggart will follow. There is no escape! *Aiiieee!*

Nature boggarts live in marshes, forests and woods, under bridges, in holes in the ground, and around sharp bends on the road, where they delight in causing serious car crashes. They kidnap small children and lead travelers astray before attacking and devouring them!

A number of locations have been named after the boggart, including Boggart Hole Clough in Manchester, England.

And if you dare to cross Boggart Bridge in Burnley, Lancashire, make sure you have a living creature to offer the Boggart or else you will forfeit your very soul!

CASE STUDY 118/59B

In the early part of the twentieth century, British animator Colt Fizzby made an ill-fated attempt to produce a black-and-white animated feature called *Bogie the Boggart*.

Beset by bad luck, the film was a commercial flop. During this period, Fizzby suffered a nervous breakdown, blaming a real boggart for all his misfortunes. "It won't leave me alone!" he had been heard to cry.

One cold winter's night, he took his dog for a walk through a local "haunted" wood, a journey they had taken many times before. Neither Fizzby nor his dog were ever seen again.

(Cinematic note: The first full-length cel animated feature film was *Snow White and the Seven Dwarfs*, released in 1937 by Walt Disney (1901–1966). The film was remarkable for also being the first animated feature both with sound and color.)

All that survives of Fizzby's film is this fragment from the musical score:

Three Cheers for Bogie
If your milk turns sour
At the midnight hour
Three cheers for Bogie!
Your window gets smashed
And your room gets trashed
It must be the Bogie!
There's a boggart in the house
He really is a louse
He makes such a racket and din
The sheets from the bed

Are torn into shreds
And all because you took him in
Three cheers for Bogie
He's the funniest spirit of them all
Three cheers for Bogie
More disgusting than a wet spitball
We shout three cheers for Bogie
'Cos if we don't he'll kill us all
So rah! Rah! Rah!
Rah! Rah! Rah!
And it's three cheers for Bogie!

HOW TO CATCH A BOGGART

Build a giant mousetrap and hide it in your bed and under the covers. When the boggart sneaks into your room to pull off the cover—SNAP!

BOGGART FACT FILE

Location: Northern England, especially around the counties of Lancashire and Yorkshire

Appearance: Hairy humanoid; any animal form

Strength: Not impressive

Weaknesses: A horseshoe hung over the front door will scare it away. Boggarts can be killed by normal means, but you then have to bury the body beside a cockerel that has had a wooden stake driven through it, under an ash tree. Even then, the boggart's spirit may return to haunt you!

Powers: Invisibility. Shape-shifter.

Fear Factor: 58.3

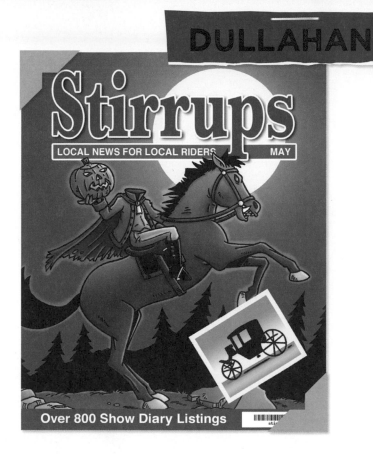

Like England, Ireland is awash with elementals and faeries, including a group of faeries known as "unseelie fairies."

Take note: There exist two prominent types of faeries. Early Scottish monster hunters categorized them as belonging either to the Seelie Court (the cheerful prankster fairies) or the Unseelie Court (the more malevolent kind).

These courts include all elemental creatures, from pixies and elves to mermaids, dragons, and giants.

In his book *Irish Fairy and Folk Tales*, published in 1888, William Butler Yeats (1865–1939), considered by many to be Ireland's greatest poet, further divided the courts into the trooping fairies and the solitary fairies.

The Trooping fairies are usually friendly, but can sometimes be cruel and nasty. Solitary

83

fairies, as the name suggests, live alone and are the more dangerous of the two sects. (There are exceptions, such as the ever-helpful brownies.)

One of the most terrifying of the solitary fairies is the Irish headless horseman, the dullahan!

The dullahan is death's herald: He only appears to those who are about to die!

Clad in a flowing black cape, his decapitated body rides astride a demonic, flamed-eyed jet-black stallion. The horse breathes sparks and hellfire as it thunders down the darkened country lanes.

The dullahan carries his head (which sometimes resembles a jack-o'-lantern) either on the saddlebow or held aloft in his hand. The eyes may either be huge or mere pinpricks of dark light, the mouth split from ear to ear in a hideous rictus grin.

The skin is smooth, the color and texture of stale dough or moldy cheese, and the entire head glows with eerie green phosphorescence that the faerie uses to light his way.

He may deliver your death notice driving a black coach known as a coach-a-bower (aka *coiste bodhar*, an Irish term meaning "silent or deaf" coach), and pulled by six headless black horses!

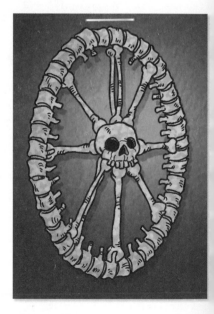

The soundless coach speeds along so fast that the undergrowth catches fire as it passes! It is decorated with candles set in human skulls and the wheel spokes are made from thighbones!

Stopping either outside of a house or at the place where a person is to die, the dullahan speaks only to call out that person's name, and when he does—BAM! It's all over for you, Jack! Upon hearing your name, your soul is violently ripped from your body and you—literally—drop dead!

CASE STUDY 600/51D

Foxhunting involves a bunch of buffoons riding on horseback and dressed in bright red costumes chasing a defenseless animal for miles across open countryside while blowing horns and shouting "tallyho!"

These morons encourage their pack of half-starved hounds to corner the fox and literally tear it to pieces while it is still conscious.

Here is an article from the popular horse magazine Stirrups, about a recent Irish foxhunt.

OUTFOXED

By Philistia Fitzwarble

What earthly delight is more joyous than hunting with hounds across the evergreen fields of Ireland?

Dogs in full cry, the ethereal sounds of the hunting horn, and the exhilarating thrill of chasing down your prey on horseback across natural fences for hour after hour.

Finally, the pleasure of watching the pack bring down the terrified animal and ravage it to shreds. There is nothing else quite like it!

Last weekend, I went out riding with the Country Gilpenny hunt. There were more than fifty of us that day, horses and riders milling around, waiting for the start. Once we had mounted up, the hounds burst away like the clappers, already picking up our quarry's scent.

Racing after them over banks and ditches, mercilessly whipping our horses to a frenzy of speed, we heard the hunt master shout, "Halloo!" The fox had been sighted! The chase was on!

Following the baying hounds, we careered over high hedgerows and across freshly planted fields, bloodlust pounding in our ears.

Ahead of the pack, I glimpsed a large red tod, running for its life! There was no escape! He was to be brought to book!

Moments before the dogs could account for Reynard, the fabled trickster fox, a chilly mist sprang up. Atop a sloping hill, I noticed a ghastly green light surrounding a rider dressed all in black.

My imagination went wild, for I believed that his horse was breathing fire and that the horseman was——headless! He held up something in his hand, some kind of large, grinning pumpkin! It was most unreal!

Our hounds let out a nerve-slicing boo-hoo before turning tail and fleeing in every direction. The horses violently reared, whinnying in mortal terror! The hunt master tried to shout over the ballyhoo, but to no avail!

Then everyone heard a piercing, ghostly voice echo down from the hill, giving name to the hunt master.

His body immediately jerked in its saddle.

Letting out an agonized cry, he clutched at his heart, toppling lifelessly from his steed, dead before he struck the ground.

Hurriedly dismounting to aid my stricken colleague, I caught sight of the fox, sitting beside the horseman.

If it were at all possible, I could swear that fox was grinning!

HOW TO CATCH DULLAHAN

Lay a trail of sugar lumps on the ground, leading into an indestructible, fireproof horse box. The dullahan's horse will not be able to resist the sweet delight. Once inside, slam shut the door! The dullahan will never again escape! (But if he does, prepare to die!)

DULLAHAN FACT FILE

Location: The Republic of Ireland
Appearance: Headless dude riding a black horse
Strength: Unearthly
Weaknesses: For such a make-you-soil-your-pants scary faerie, he is absolutely terrified of anything gold, even a tiny hat pin! Da wimp. (But don't tell him we said that!)
Powers: Death (like, what other powers do you need?!)
Fear Factor: 89.8

And cue our audience:

"*Fairies*?!! Ya kiddin', right? We're hard-core monster hunters!"

Oh, ye of little faith!

Trust us. Cute fairies don't rock our particular boat either. We're more interested in the wicked, vicious, and downright evil type, what some paranormal investigators brand as . . . dark fairies!

The term *faerie* (aka fairy, faery, fayerye, feirie, fay, or fae) means both an enchanted realm and also the supernatural creatures that inhabit such lands. It once described all magical creatures and not simply those pip-squeaks that prance around a toadstool ring at the bottom of the garden.

Being "nature" creatures, you'll mostly find fairies hanging out in woods and forests, inside caves, behind rocks and hills, and beside ponds, rivers, and waterfalls.

And these fiendish fae exist worldwide! In almost *every* country!

Until the Victorian Age (a period of British history named after the reign of Queen Victoria, which lasted from 1837–1901), fairies flew without wings, flying instead on ragwort stems or on the backs of birds. When they realized that humans thought wings were awesome cool, they added them to their fashion accessories.

While "good" fairies take pleasure in tangling a sleeping child's hair, opening the freezer door, stealing small but precious items, or leading nighttime travelers astray, dark fairies take this meanness one step further.

These creeps get their kicks by riding animals to exhaustion and forcing teenage humans to dance all night until their bodies shrivel away through lack of sleep.

They kidnap babies and replace them with changelings (fairies disguised as the victim), and give humans the truly horrific disease of tuberculosis.

(Medical note: Tuberculosis or TB—short for *tubercle bacillus*—is a deadly, infectious disease that can be passed on by coughs and sneezes. It attacks the lungs and other parts of the body. One-third of the world's population is thought to be infected with tuberculosis, with new infections occurring at the rate of roughly one per second. Approximately 50 percent of all those infected will die of the disease, and more than 1.5 million deaths result every year, mostly in developing countries.)

Fairies, dark or otherwise, will quite happily kill you if you upset them.

Chopping down thorn trees is a definite no-no, as is digging in faerie hills and faerie forts.

Sharpening knives or iron tools on a Friday should be avoided because this offends not only fairies but the entire race of fae.

Also, don't take a sieve out after dark; or a hot meal, unless it is sprinkled with salt.

If you do—ZAP! You've been warned!

CASE STUDY 224/66F

Project Blue Book was a study of unidentified flying objects (UFOs) led by the United States Air Force that began in 1952 and ended in 1969. Of the 12,618 sightings that were investigated, 701 of them were considered to be "unexplained."

During this time, a second study—ingeniously titled Project Green Book—was set up by the clandestine government department known as the Research Intelligence Center.

This was to determine whether sightings of fairies and elementals were real, and what threat they posed to national security.

Here is one of those reports!

PROJECT GREEN BOOK

SPECIAL REPORT NO.23

FOR OFFICIAL USE ONLY
APRIL 12 - 1967

THE RESEARCH INTELLIGENCE CENTER

*****

CLASSIFIED
IF FOUND RETURN TO U.S. GOVERNMENT

INVESTIGATION OF FAERIE EVENTS AT CATSKILL PARK, NY, ON APRIL 12, 1967

On Wednesday, April 12, a report came in from a hiker who was travelling with a companion through the 700,000-acre forest reserve known as Catskill Park, an area that borders New York's Catskill Mountains.

The man, a Mr. Bull Loney, claims that the men were traveling in a southwest direction at 9:47 a.m. precisely, when they saw bright lights ahead of them and the sound of, in his words, "tinkling laughter."

Approaching with caution, they came upon a small clearing.

On the dry, dusty ground, they spotted what appeared to be tiny footprints. Lying close by was a teeny red hat and a miniature fishing pole.

Glancing up, small, bright lights danced over their heads.

"It were then that Ah realized t'werent no lights but actual li'l people wit' glistenin' wings," Loney later told investigators. "Theys was talkin' in a mite weird language. Me 'n' my pal Will, we wuz plumb amazed!"

According to Loney, Will pulled out his camera to snap a photograph of the creatures, "t'sell to that there national daily, th' *Weekly World Examiner*. Will reckoned theys would pay plenty fer such a pikture!" said Loney.

It was then that the creatures noticed the men. Holding up "tiny fizzing sticks," they pointed them at Will, and "POOF! He, like, disappeared!"

Loney claimed that he ran for his life.

Once home, he reported his encounter to the authorities, who immediately contacted the Research Intelligence Center.

Investigators were dispatched to the area, but no evidence of these creatures was discovered. Will remains missing, and at this time, no explanation for his disappearance can be offered.

WHAT TO DO WITH A FAERIE

Sneak up behind one. Ring a bell very loudly, knocking it unconscious. Then tie it to the top of your Christmas tree in miniature iron manacles—better than a plastic faerie, any day!

FAERIE FACT FILE

Location: The world
Appearance: Tiny humanoid creatures with or without gossamer wings
Strength: Physical strength—puny. Magical strength—impressive.
Weaknesses: Iron, bells, loud whistling (pathetic!), turning your clothes inside out, leaping over water (especially one that is southward-flowing), fire, bread, oatmeal, four-leaf clovers, daisies, Saint-John's-wort, red-berried trees, the Bible, holy crosses and other religious symbols, magical spells, and urine! (Sprinkle copious amounts of pee around your house to keep away fairies . . . not to mention all of your friends!) A horseshoe hung over the front door and a nail driven into the body of a cow that has fallen over a cliff will also work wonders.
Powers: Magic, flight, shape-shifters
Fear Factor: 67.5

The juvenile delinquents of the goblin set, these creatures make Krampus seem almost tame!

Imagine the nastiest, most bad-tempered, vile, disgusting, violent, and vicious fae possible, and you have the Kallikantzaroi! (Oh, and they smell terrible!)

They run riot at night through towns and villages in Greece and Cyprus during the twelve days of Christmas (December 25–January 5), screaming and hollering, smashing windows, ripping up gardens, destroying vehicles, and oftentimes slicing and dicing animals and humans!

Luckily, they're incredibly dim! For the best part of every year, they spend all their time underground sawing through the world tree so that it will collapse and destroy the Earth.

What's the world tree? Glad you asked!

Many religions practiced by the native people of North America, Siberia, and Indo-European nations believe that there exists a colossal tree whose branches support the heavens. (So we're talking *ginormous* here!)

The world tree connects the heavens with Earth and the underworld.

Anyway, the dumb Kallikantzaroi are moments away from sawing through the world tree when Christmas arrives, and they head for the surface to *paaaarrrr-taaaayyy*!!

Unfortunately, by the time they remember the world tree and rush back underground to finish their task, it's too late. The world tree has completely healed itself and they have to start sawing through it, all over again! During this twelve-day period, no one is safe. The Kallikantzaroi will break into your home through the front door or down the chimney and go on a rampage, breaking all the furniture, eating all the food, and leaving the occupants half-dead either through violence or fear!

Thankfully, these dumb creatures are relatively easy to chase off.

For starters, mark your front door with a black cross on Christmas Eve, or burn some incense or a pair of old shoes indoors. (After first sticking a clothespin over your nose!)

A black-handled knife, a handful of salt, a blazing fire (to stop them from coming down the chimney), hanging the lower jaw of a pig behind the front door, or placing sweetmeats, pork bones, or sausages inside the chimney, should also do the trick.

Failing that, wait until the eve of the Epiphany (January 6), when village priests sprinkle holy water mixed with sweet basil around the streets to mark the end of the twelve days of Christmas.

The Kallikantzaroi are terrified of the stuff and skedaddle back underground for another year.

Boxing Day found us at the North Pole, celebrating Christmas in an elf house, which is somewhat similar to an alehouse—a pub to the Brits, Irish, Aussies, New Zealanders, and Canucks among you—but with a lot more elves!

Two such elves were knocking back the powerful mulled wine and grumbling about the problems they'd had in helping Santa deliver presents to a village in Greece.

Recognizing an "exclusive" when we hear one, we slyly recorded the conversation on our smartphone for all our monster hunter pals.

Think of it as an early Christmas present!

THE DWARF & HOBBIT ELFHOUSE, NORTH POLE, DECEMBER 26

TRANSCRIPT BEGINS:

CLICK

[Background noise of raucous laughing and shouting]

ELF I: Man, whats a night! I is shattereds!

ELF 2: Y'r not wrong there, Lumpy! Shift 42 was, like, y'know, the worst! It was, yeah, horrend[voice drowned out by laughter]

LUMPY: We's would get the Greece job! Didja sees all those rotten Kallikant[loud shouting], Dumpy? Theres was hundreds of thems! Screamins and holler[garbled] and tearing ups the pla[drowned out by loud dwarf bodily noises and much laughter]!

DUMPY: Santa should have, like, yeah, y'know, warned us about them pesky gobli[piano music starts up in the background, dialogue drowned out by a chorus of "Rudolph the Red-Nosed Reindeer"]

[music dies off]

DUMPY: . . . 'n' y'shoulda, y'know, seen what "present" they left in, like, the punch bowl! EWWWWW!

[The door opens and jingle bells ring followed by a hearty "HO-HO-HO!"]

LUMPY: Well, if it's nots the Big Mans him[drowned out by another "HO-HO!"]

DUMPY: Too many, like, yeah, mince pies, that's his, y'know, problem! [cruel elfish laughter]

LUMPY: Buts he's nots so's big in Greece, Dumps. Theys start their Christ[garbled] present-givings on Decembers 6, the Feast of Saint Nicholas, to be sure. But thens again on Januarys I, which is the Feast of Saint Basil, whos is *Greece's* Father Christmas! Ole Saint Nick is onlys the Greeks Patron Saint of Sailors! *[drunken elfish giggles]* Fatso here, hes hates that! Ha-Ha!

DUMPY: Yeah, wadda, y'know, come down fer 'im! *[drunken elfish giggles]* Still, I'm glad it's over for, like *[HIC!]*, another year. Those Kolly . . . Keellee . . . Kull . . . them, y'know, gobby goblums are gonna give me *[garbled]*mares for *[HIC!]* weeks!

LUMPY: Don't reminds *[HIC!]* me, Dumpy! If Santa tries sending us backs to that *[drowned out by raucous laughter]* next years, I is *[HIC!]* quittin'! Hes can stuffs his job! Elfs benefits or no *[HIC!]* elfs benefits!

DUMPY: *[voice slurred]* MERRY, y'know, CHRISTMAS, LUMPY! *[HIC!]*

LUMPY: Ands to *[voice slurred]*, pals! Ands *[garbled]* you! *[HIC!]*

KALLIKANTZAROI FACT FILE

Location: Greece and Cyprus
Appearance: Hideously ugly and bestial, tall or short with a dark olive complexion. Huge head; glaring red eyes; ears similar to a goat or donkey; lolling bloodred tongue; ferocious boar tusks; lanky monkey arms with long, curved fingernails; cloven hooves; and a black, fur-covered body.
Strength: Immensely strong!
Weaknesses: Aside from those already listed, leave a colander on the porch. The Kallikantzaroi can't resist counting all the holes, but being fatheads, they can only count to two. This keeps them busy until sunrise, when they have to flee from the light.
Powers: Thug power!
Fear Factor: 33.3

GENIUS USE FOR KALLIKANTZAROI

Use them as test subjects in police riot-control training!

Humans have been extracting valuable minerals and metals from the earth for tens of thousands of years.

The Lion Cave mine in Swaziland, southern Africa, dates back more than 43,000 years! It was here that hematite (a mineral form of iron (III) oxide, otherwise known as Fe_2O_3—but heck, you knew that!) was mined to make the pigment red ochre. (Ochre is a naturally occurring colored clay.)

The ochre was used by people of the Upper Paleolithic period (or "Late Stone Age," a period lasting from approximately 38,000 to 8000 BC) to paint the walls of their caves, their tools, and even their own skin. (Yep, they were the world's first tattoo artists—sort of.)

And what does any of this have to do with faerie folk? Quite a lot, actually!

The very moment that the first mine was excavated, the knockers appeared.

These wizened dwarfs stand two feet tall and are often greenish in color. They used to be especially prevalent in Cornwall and Devon in England, where mining began around 2100 BC in the early Bronze Age, and finally ended in 1998.

Knockers have also been seen in Wales (where they are called bwca), Australia (knackers, which, by the way, is how the word *knockers* is pronounced!), America (tommyknockers), and Germany (*berggeister* or *bergmännlein*, meaning "mountain ghosts" or "little miners").

The name comes from their habit of knocking on mine walls moments before a cave-in. Some knockers are good-hearted spirits, knocking to warn miners of impending disaster or to lead them to a rich vein of ore.

Others are downright malicious and deadly!

If they feel neglected or disrespected by humans, or hear whistling or swearing (both of which greatly offends them), their vindictive streak takes over.

They will dig up rocks for miners to trip over; sabotage machinery; fill the shaft with poisonous gas; flood the mine from an underground river; or knock out support posts, causing the roof to collapse, which traps, injures, or kills those inside.

When a mine has been "played out" and closed down, knockers may prefer to find alternative work.

Many a family disaster or death has been foretold by a mysterious knocking on the front door!

CASE STUDY 134/34K

Fifteen-year-old Soul-Gon McDonald of Wollongong, New South Wales, Australia, has kindly allowed us to reproduce one of the entries in her monster-hunter diary.

January 12

G'day, Diary!

My Yank cobber Toby told me to take a geek at a silver pit mine deep in th' bush, one that had been abandoned since Cocky was an egg.

He'd heard on th' bush telegraph that th' place was haunted by a knacker!

So spot on th' sparrow's beak 'n' before th' oldies resurfaced, I hit th' frog 'n' toad 'n' headed out for th' Never Never to take a Captain Cook for meself.

Sixteen clicks later 'n' I was within cooie o' th' woop-woop.

Th' mine was boarded up, but a few taps from my nulla nulla soon sorted that out.

I went in deep, fossickin' around. Rustin' tools o' the trade lay scattered about 'n' th' silence was deafenin'!

After half an hour o' stumblin' around 'n' continually whackin' my noggin on the low ceilin' I was feelin' a bit blue duck 'n' mondo maggoty toward Tobias!

I was about to head back when my torchlight caught twin red eyes glarin' at me from th' darkness.

This gruff voice boomed out: "Abandon hope all ye who enter here!"

From behind a rock leaped out this tiny codger with green skin, a wizened dial, full face fungus—and wearin' a miner's helmet!

I stared at him like a stunned mullet! It was a ridgie-didge knacker! Grouse!

"G'day, sport!" I said. "How ya doin'?"

In reply, th' yahoo pulled out a nasty-lookin' stone hammer 'n' ran straight at me!

I was seriously in th' cactus! Ahhh!

97

Tryin' not to cack my dacks, I swung my nulla nulla, 'n' demolished a support post. *BAMM!*

Suddenly, th' mine was full o' loud knockin'! That was my cue to run like a stint!

Reachin' th' entrance, I leapt like billyo, landin' on th' sandy ground as th' mine collapsed behind me! *CRRRAAASSSH!*

Even stevens, that's one knacker that won't be any more bother! Bonza!

For those of you not well-versed in Aussie speak, here are some translations of Soul-Gon's diary entry:

G'day: Hello
Cobber: friend
Geek: a look
Bush: the Outback
Since Cocky was an egg: a long time ago
Bush telegraph: the rumor and gossip grapevine
Sparrow's beak: daybreak
The frog and toad: the road
Never-Never: the Outback
Captain Cook: look
Click: 0.6 m/1 km
With cooie: nearby
Woop-woop: remote location
Nullu nulla: Aboriginal heavy wooden club
Fossick around: to search aimlessly
Noggin: skull
Blue duck: disappointed
Codger: old man
Dial: face
Face fungus: beard
Ridgie-didge: the genuine article
Grouse: cool, awesome
Yahoo: unruly or bad-tempered person
In the cactus: in trouble
Cack the dacks: to dirty one's underwear
Run like a stint: to run very fast
Billyo: with great speed or gusto
Even stevens: equal or odds-on chance
Bonza: excellent

KNOCKERS FACT FILE

Location: Cornwall and Wales, UK; Australia, Germany, United States
Appearance: Wrinkly little green-skinned dwarfs dressed as miners
Strength: Powerful
Weaknesses: None
Powers: Can foretell death and disaster (but only because they tend to cause it!)
Fear Factor: 45.8 (If you are a miner; the rest of us are laughing! Well, until there's a knock at the front door, that is! Eek!)

WHAT TO DO WITH AN UNEMPLOYED KNOCKER

Hire him to give your history teacher a wake-up call, every hour on the hour, all through the night! Your teacher will be so tired, he'll fall asleep in class and you'll enjoy a free period!

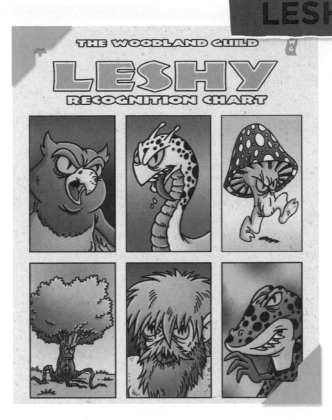

If you go down to the woods
today, you're sure of a big surprise
If you go down to the woods
today, you'd better go in disguise . . .
. . . otherwise, the leshy might getcha!

(Musical note: The melody for the original "Teddy Bear's Picnic" was written in 1907 by American composer John Walter Bratton, and the lyrics added in 1932 by Irish songwriter Jimmy Kennedy.)

Derived from the Slavic word *les,* meaning *forest,* leshy are male woodland spirits who protect all fauna and flora of the forests. Magical in nature, these dudes are shape-shifters to the nth degree (i.e., the maximum amount).

Mondo-powerful, they can transform themselves into the tallest trees or the smallest blades of grass, as well as any kind of bird, animal, or insect.

For a laugh, the mischievous leshy will sometimes frighten off humans by appearing as a large, talking mushroom!

(Botany note: Mushrooms are the fleshy, fruiting body of a fungus. There are more than 38,000 known varieties of mushrooms worldwide, many deadly poisonous! So if you see one in a field our advice is DON'T TOUCH! You never know, it might be a leshy in cunning disguise!)

Recognized as the King of the Forest, the leshy will normally appear as an extremely tall man with hair and beard made of living grass and vines; huge, fiery-green bugged-out eyes; and pale white skin and blue cheeks, which is a consequence of his blue blood.

He sometimes adds grass for body hair, horns, a tail, and hooves for good measure—and always carries a big club.

If you go leshy-hunting, do remember that these are not evil creatures. They love animals and want to protect the environment.

They care for all living things, even humans. They protect the crops and animals of farmers and shepherds, and if you befriend a leshy, he will gladly show you the secrets of his magic.

Before entering the forest, say a protective prayer and leave out some bread, salt, candy, or cookies, and the religious cross from around your neck, and you and the leshy will be lifelong buds!

It is the destructive, unthinking humans the leshy have a craving for, and who can blame them?! Evil hunters of animals (and also fishermen) are the number one target for these faerie powerhouses.

Appear in a forest with gun or rod, and chances are, you aren't coming out again!

The leshy will remove path signs or imitate the voice of someone you know, luring you back to his cave where he will make you extremely sick until you choke on your own vomit. (Nice.)

Or else—he'll tickle you to death! (Being soft-hearted, a leshy likes his victims to die laughing!)

Extremely territorial, they will fight and chase off other leshy who enter their turf. Fallen trees in forests attest to such momentous battles!

CASE STUDY 045/22L

WOODLAND GUILD
Junior Woodland Rangers

This card certifies that:

Ranger Rich

is a member in good standing of
The Junior Wodland Rangers.

Ranger Rich
SIGNED

Ranger Rich is the leader of the Junior Woodland Rangers chapter of the Woodland Guild.

He has kindly allowed us to reprint his open letter to all members of the JWR that appears in his latest publication, the Leshy Recognition Chart.

Hello chums!

It's your ole pal Ranger Rich here with another one of my fun-packed recognition charts!

This time, I'll be showing you how to tell a leshy from a cow pat!

I first came across a leshy on my recent busman's holiday to Slovenia.

This country is a Woodland Ranger's dream! Over 58 percent of the country is forested.

There are forests in the lowlands and hills, the uplands and mountains. Forests as far as the eye can see!

One percent of all the Earth's living creatures live here and 2 percent of land and freshwater creatures.

The woodlands are packed with great animals, like the wolf, the lynx, and the brown bear, the largest wild animal in Europe. And plants and trees galore.

But some turned out not to be native fauna and flora, but leshy in cunning disguise!

Leshy are shape-shifting woodland spirits, and you have to be very careful not to upset them!

Unfortunately, I did just that when he was walking through the Pravljiŏni gozd (Slovene for "Magic Forest," a forest that lies on the slopes above Lake Bohinj) and accidentally stepped on a small *Amanita muscaria*, or fly agaric mushroom.

Only this wasn't a "red cap with white spots" mushroom at all, but a leshy who was out sunbathing! Oops!

Snarling bestially, he immediately shape-shifted into a giant beech tree and tried to flatten me with his thick branches!

Well, I took to my heels and ran as fast as I could and somehow managed to escape!

And with this cool chart, if you go trekking in a Slovenian forest, you'll be able to recognize a leshy when you see one!

Your Pal,

Ranger Rich!

Ranger Rich

WHAT TO DO WITH A LESHY

Take the leshy and a large group of people to a recording studio and have him tickle them almost to death. Sell the recording to a TV production company as "canned laughter" for their comedy shows!

LESHY FACT FILE

Location: Slavic countries, including Russia, Poland, Serbia, Slovakia, Bulgaria, et al

Appearance: If it's an animal, vegetable, or mineral, it could be a leshy!

Strength: Magically powerful

Weaknesses: Turn your clothes inside out and put them on backward, then place your shoes on the opposite feet. The leshy will give you Total Respect and let you go!

Powers: Shape-shifting

Fear Factor: 56

Drop-dead gorgeous half-woman (top half), half-fish (bottom half), these totally evil fae have been drowning humans at least as early as 1000 BC, where they are mentioned in cuneiform writing on Assyrian clay tablets.

They have been sighted throughout history and worldwide, in oceans, rivers, and lakes.

The seafaring ancient Greeks had run-ins with these murderous merfolk. So did the Vikings. And Chinese sailors have seen mermaids who *wept tears that became pearls.*

The Japanese believe that if you catch and eat a mermaid, it will grant you immortality.

In Warsaw, the capital of Poland, their coat of arms depicts a mermaid holding a shield and sword.

The term *mermaid* comes from the Old English words *mere* (sea) and *maid* (teenage girl or young woman).

On January 4, 1493, famed Genoan (person from the now-defunct Republic of Genoa, what is today northwest Italy) explorer, navigator, and colonizer Christoffa Corombo (aka Christopher Columbus, who was born in 1451 and died in 1506), was sailing off the coast of Hispaniola, a small island in the Caribbean, when he spotted three mermaids who *"rose high out of the sea, but were not as beautiful as they are represented."*

English explorer and navigator Henry Hudson (1565–1611), who sailed to North America four times and has the Hudson River, Bay, and Strait named after him, sighted a mermaid in Russian waters on June 15, 1608, and described her as having a *"tail like a porpoise and speckled like a macrell* (mackerel).*"*

These soulless harridans of the deep prey on sailors, fishermen, and swimmers, entrancing them with their hypnotic singing.

Men will swim far out to sea or steer their ship toward a mermaid waiting on a rock, and then be pulled under the water to drown.

But their intense wickedness doesn't stop there! Oh, no! After dragging the victim down to her opulent kingdom on the ocean floor, the mermaid will devour him (yep, these ladies are man-eaters!) before trapping his soul inside a cage forevermore!

CASE STUDY 200/64M

The award-winning kids' wildlife show It's *A Wild Wild World* is hosted by popular young presenters Carrie Boo and Al Paca. A recent *IAWWW* special featured Carrie's hunt for the mythological mermaid!

Here is an excerpt from the TV show in script form:

CONEY ISLAND MERMAID PARADE—WIDE
Track on passing floats of mermaids, mermen, and merchildren in colorful
costumes, interspersed with CU of smiling spectators. Fade up audio

                    PRESENTER—CARRIE BOO (VO)
         New York's annual Coney Island Mermaid Parade takes
         place on the first Saturday after summer solstice.
         Hundreds of people dressed as merfolk—and more
         than half a million spectators—descend upon
         the city to celebrate the start of summer.

Cut across to presenter in f/g of shot, speaking into mic

                         PRESENTER
         Why do mermaids hold such a powerful
         attraction for people, even after thousands
         of years? And do they really exist?

Tight CU of presenter, smiling TC
                         PRESENTER
              Yes, viewers! They do! As
              you're about to find out!

CUT TO:
PHOENIX ISLANDS, PACIFIC OCEAN—AERIAL SHOT
Slo-mo track across atolls and coral reefs

                       PRESENTER (OC)
         I've come to the Phoenix Islands in the
         Pacific Ocean: eight atolls and two coral reefs
         of pristine ecosystems that remain
         untouched by human hands.

CUT TO:

BOAT—EXT
Presenter stands up in bow of sailing boat, speaking TC. In the background
is a large rock pushing up out of the water

PRESENTER

Sailors claim to have seen a
mermaid in this area only recently.
A large wave smashes against the rock.

Track in tight to show a mermaid with golden hair now sitting on the rock,
combing her golden hair

PRESENTER (OC)
(squealing) And there's one right there! Oh my gosh!
Quick, Stuart! Tight shot! (shouting) Now, gosh darn it!
I mean . . . (excited) yes, viewers, this is a mermaid,
a creature never before captured on film! It's an It's A
Wild Wild World exclusive!

Tight CU of mermaid. She begins to sing

PRESENTER (OC)
(gasps) Oooh! Wh-what a beautiful
voice . . . so . . . hypnotic . . . feel so . . . so . . . sleepy . . .

A huge school of fish leaps up out of the water, filling the camera lens

PRESENTER (OC)
(screams) Aaaaah! We're being attacked!
Oww! Get off! Help! Cut! Cut! Aiiiieeee!
(screams fade)

FADE OUT

Glossary of Script Terms
AERIAL SHOT: a shot taken from a
crane, plane, balloon, etc., looking
down on the scene from a certain
height
CUT ACROSS: a quick cut to the
subject in the same scene
CU: close-up of subject
CUT: stop filming
CUT TO: cut away to a new location
EXT: exterior or outside location.
(Also, INT is an interior or indoor
location.)
FADE OUT: screen fades to black,
indicating the end of the film
FADE UP: when the sound is slowly
turned up

F/G: foreground
MIC: microphone
OC: off-camera; where a subject is
at the scene but cannot be seen. Also
known as OOS (out of shot)
SLO-MO: slow motion track of the
camera
TC: to camera; a subject speaking
straight to the camera
TRACK: to pan across; to follow an
action or reveal a scene
VO: voice-over; when a subject is
recording the narrative after the
film has been shot
WIDE: a wide shot of the entire scene

MERMAID FACT FILE

WHAT TO DO WITH
A CAPTURED MERMAID

Rope her to the front of a sailing
ship and use her as a really cool
figurehead!

Location: Rivers, lakes, seas, and oceans of the
world
Appearance: Half-human, half-fish
Strength: Average to powerful, depending on size.
Weaknesses: Susceptible to any conventional
weapon (a harpoon through the head should do the
trick!)
Powers: Possibly immortal. Hypnotic singing.
Weather control. Able to predict weather patterns.
Fear Factor: 57.3

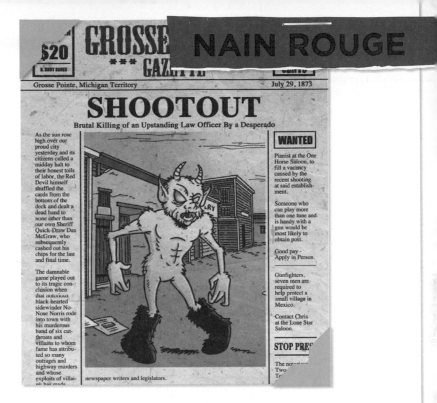

Le Nain Rouge, to give him his full appellation, is French for "the Red Dwarf."

This is because this evil hobgoblin originated in Normandy, France. He then popped over to the United States in 1701 with French aristocrat, explorer, adventurer, and military commander Antoine Laumet de la Mothe, sieur (Sir) de Cadillac (1658–1730).

The first white settler to the area, Laumet founded Fort Pontchartrain du Détroit, aka Fort Détroit, on the *Rivière du Détroit* (Detroit River). This later developed into the great industrial city that we know today.

Out for an evening walk with his wife, Laumet had a nasty run in with the Nain Rouge. Attacking the fae with his cane, the Frenchman chased him off, and the Nain Rouge bitterly cursed him.

Three years later, Laumet's luck went belly-up. He lost his entire fortune and ended up in prison! (Never tick off an unseelie faerie! They hold a *looooooong* grudge!)

And the ever-vindictive Nain Rouge has been messing with the people of Detroit ever since!

He is described as being a red-skinned, impish dwarf, with hideous gnarled features, a matted fur body, blazing red eyes, rotting teeth, and a maniacal grin.

Dressed in red or black fur boots, he emits a freaky-deaky cry similar to that of a cawing crow.

A dreaded omen to the onset of misfortune, destruction, and death to Detroit citizens, the Nain Rouge has made many an impressionable appearance over the centuries.

In 1763, the Native American Chief Pontiac (real name Obwandiyag; born circa 1720, and died in 1769), leader of the Ottawa tribe, started a three-year rebellion against the settlers.

One of his biggest victories came in July, 1763 as about 250 British troops attempted a surprise attack on his camp near Fort Détroit. Pontiac, however, had been alerted to the attack and slaughtered the British soldiers as they approached.

It is said that the creek (or *run*) close to the fort ran red with blood for many days, and the horrific attack would forevermore be known as the Battle of Bloody Run. The Nain Rouge was observed gleefully watching the slaughter, dancing on the banks of the Detroit River.

He was eyeballed multiple times before the terrible fire that swept through Detroit on the morning of June 11, 1805. The conflagration was so great that almost the entire city was destroyed.

Yet another sighting of the evil faerie heralded the surrender of Fort Detroit to the British on August 16, 1812, during the War of 1812.

Nain Rouge was seen just before the Detroit Race Riot of June 20, 1943, which lasted three days at the cost of thirty-four lives.

And again before the even worse Detroit Riot of 1967, a five-day race riot that started on Sunday, July 23. This civil uprising left forty-three people dead, 467 injured, and more than one thousand buildings destroyed.

And when the deadly ice storm of 1976 struck the city, guess who was there to celebrate?!

But the people of Detroit are a hardy lot.

Each year in March, on the Sunday after the spring equinox (March 20), the city holds a colorful (and noisy!) carnival called *La Marche du Nain Rouge*.

People dress up as the Nain Rouge and march through the streets, driving the evil spirit from the city and back to the spirit plane for another year! Go, Detroiters!

CASE STUDY 868/5NR

The Wild West was so-called because, well, heck, it sure was wild! Bank, railroad, and stagecoach robberies; cattle rustling; horse stealing; landgrabs; saloon brawls; and racial violence were the norm, and daily shootings and lynchings left the dusty streets stained with blood.

No more so than the ever-expanding city of Detroit, Michigan. This article was published by the *Grosse Point Gazette* on July 29, 1873. (Read the front page of the newspaper before continuing the thrilling story here!)

SHOOTOUT (cont.)

Norris had set his gun sights on holding up and robbing the city's Silver Dollar Bank. McGraw had no intentions of letting him do so.

At one minute past high noon, the combatants met on the field of battle at opposite ends of the street.

Terrified citizens ran for cover as the two parties stepped forward ten paces, the spurs on their heels clinking with every step.

"Norris," drawled McGraw. "You're under arrest."

"Sheriff, go to h——!" spat back Norris, the gang reaching immediately for their holstered weapons.

A terrible gunfight ensued, and when the smoke cleared, all seven bandits were lying dead or mortally wounded. McGraw isn't called Quick-Draw for nothing.

"Shoot no more," wheezed Norris, his hand pressed against a gaping hole in his gut. "I am dead."

It was then that tragedy brought down the curtain after its final act.

Our brave sheriff was momentarily distracted by a bizarre red creature that ran out from behind the saloon and started dancing on the bodies of the brigands, giggling freakishly.

Norris saw his chance and fired his gun one final time before expiring in the dirt beneath which his remains would soon be interred.

A lucky shot, no doubt, although not for Sheriff Quick-Draw McGraw. The bullet passed clean through his temple and out the other side.

Another victim of this fair city's greatest nemesis, the Nain Rouge.

DRAW, PARD'NER!

HOW TO STOP THE NAIN ROUGE

Trick him into breaking a mirror and giving *himself* seven years' bad luck!

NAIN FACT FILE

Location: Detroit, Michigan
Appearance: Ugly red critter
Strength: Average
Weaknesses: Carnivals
Powers: Bad-luck curse. Anyone who meets the Nain Rouge is guaranteed to be in for one heck of a lousy day!
Fear Factor: If you're a Detroiter, we're figuring at least 60.1

SALAMANDER

And we're not talking about those 550-plus species of colorful amphibians that look like lizards and are unique for being the only vertebrate (an animal with a spinal column or backbone) capable of regenerating lost limbs.

Whaddya think this is—a wildlife study?! Get real!

Nah, we're much more interested in the mentally vicious and insane elemental beings of the same name that are made entirely of . . . fire!

Word up. The salamander is the most powerful of all the four elementals, so only the most experienced of monster hunters should think about tackling one!

Their leader is the terrifying flame being known as Djinn (not to be confused with the Middle Eastern demon of the same name), who was born in the heart of the sun and appeared on Earth as it first took form 4.54 billion years ago. So, y'know, the dude's kinda old.

Whenever a flame appears, whether by matchstick or blazing inferno, a salamander is there to bring it to life. They create all things associated with fire and heat, including destructive lightning strikes and exploding volcanoes!

Natural shape-shifters, they can appear in many forms and sizes, from small balls of fire to human-form flame beings, but their personal preference is that of a small fire-lizard or a huge fire-dragon.

That ancient Roman know-it-all, Pliny the Elder (AD 23–79; a guy who seemed to have an opinion on just about *everything*!) mentioned the salamander in his writings.

Commenting on the elemental's merciless powers, Pliny wrote: *"It spits out a milky matter from its mouth, and whatever part of the human body is touched with this, all the hairs fall off, and the part assumes the appearance of leprosy."*

(Medical note: Leprosy is a nasty infectious disease caused by the bacteria *Mycobacterium leprae* that attacks the human nervous system, especially the face, hands, and feet. It was first described by the ancient Egyptians, around 1550 BC. Even today, almost 200,000 people suffer from the debilitating illness, especially in underdeveloped countries of Africa, Asia, and Latin America.)

Apart from making your hair fall out, the salamander's body is so pumping with juicy poisons that if it wraps itself around a fruit tree and you eat from it, you instantly drop dead! (So no snacking on the job!)

Interesting to note: Although they are fire demons and made from flame, their bodies are so intensely cold that they have the ability to extinguish any fire, no matter how large!

Especially prevalent in Arab, Asian, and African countries, these supernatural-fueled pyromaniacs are regularly called upon by wizards and witches to destroy their enemies!

CASE STUDY 336/88S

We proudly present another one of the straight-up hard-as-cheese-balls thrill-chill adventures of everyone's favorite sixteenth-century Franciscan monster-fightin' monk, Brother Jacob!

The Adventures of Brother Jacob

THE ADVENTURES OF BROTHER JACOB

My religious pilgrimage to spread understanding of the good Lord's most sacred texts brought me at last to the golden shores of the wild African continent, and the cursed earth of the Sahara Desert.

By my trowth, ne'r have I seen before or after a place of such desolation! Only hell itself could look so grim! Five days into my travels and the burning sands did blister my bare feet most harshly.

The relentless heat of purgatory washed down upon my holy habit, which I refused to cast off for wont of offending the Creator of All Things.

T'was at the moment that my nasal passages were assaulted most ferociously by an odor of utter foul origin!

Glancing yonder, I gave notice upon a tree vigorously burning little ways ahead! God's teeth! Could this be a message from the Divine Presence to his most fervent servant?

I proposed to approach that fiery palm when all but a sudden it transmogrified into a hideous, fire-breathing lizard!

"Thou art a swine, sirrah!" I spake angrily. "To attempt such a foolishness of me thus! Prithee, what is it thou dost want?"

"Only thine death, human!" hissed the one whom immediately I realized was naught if not the deadly elemental salamander!

With that, did battle commence!

With blood boiling from both heat and righteous fury, I parried and thrust my sacred sword seraph against yon salamander's attacks, from midday to eventide, with neither combatant triumphing o'er the other!

"Curse thee, human!" wept at last the wearied elemental. "Fall, whyeth not thee?"

"Upon Judgment Day only shalt I rest!" I cried, forcing my screaming limbs to make one final assault.

With pounding heart, I leaped above the creature's blazing barrage and ascended its strangely freezing-cold body to stand upon its neck!

"Die, brute beast of Beelzebub!" I bellowed, plunging the seraph into the salamander's right eye. "Diiiiieeeeee!"

There followed a most blinding flash of incandescent hellfire, and thine Lord's faithful servant lost all consciousness.

Reviving, I thus found myself the guest of a tribe of wandering nomads, who were kindly taking me to the nearest village for much-needed respite.

I had been found hanging from the hilt of my sword, which was wedged high in a tall palm tree. The fellows believed me to have attacked yon tree during a bout of sunstroke!

I alone knew the truth. The Ambassador of Divine Wrath had triumphed, once more!

Hallelujah!

WHAT TO DO WITH A SALAMANDER

Invite a salamander over for a garden party, and rope him in to light your barbecue—just don't upset him; otherwise, the food might not be the only thing char-grilled!

SALAMANDER FACT FILE

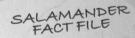

Location: Africa, Asia, the Middle East, South and North America, Europe

Appearance: Flame dudes!

Strength: Able to destroy entire kingdoms without much effort

Weaknesses: Yeah, well . . .

Powers: Flame and heat. Shape-shifters.

Fear Factor: 96.4

This evil and vindictive Slavic water elemental gets his kicks outta drowning humans and stealing their souls, which he keeps in quaint, porcelain lid-covered cups.

Porcelain—china to you and us, so named because of the country it originated from—was first made in China—in a primitive form during the Tang Dynasty (618–907) and in the form best known in the West during the Yuan Dynasty (1279–1368).

In polite vodníci (plural of vodník) society, the more soul cups a vodník owns, the better his wealth and status among his peers. (Monster Hunter Tip of the Day: To release a soul, one must lift the cup lid, allowing the spirit to float, in the form of a bubble, back to the surface.)

When hunting a vodník, head for ponds, fast-flowing rivers, or swamps, and keep a sharp eye out for a naked, green-skinned old man who is covered in black scales or fur, with long, green hair and beard; glowing red eyes; horns; and a fish's tail.

He's coated in algae, has webbed paws, and occasionally appears riding on a half-sunk log, making loud splashes as he travels along.

Or he may look like an unshaven, short old man with green skin and gills, and wearing a green suit and boater hat with long, speckled ribbons. (You can tell there's a vodník around by the puddles left from water dripping from his coattails.)

Then again, don't take any chances with a blue-skinned old man with a white beard and gray hair. Oh, and he appears younger or older, depending on the waxing and waning of the moon.

Solitary creatures, vodníci spend their days sitting on rocks, playing card games.

They will gladly play with humans, but take care, because these twisted creatures are seriously bad losers!

If you win, they'll take revenge by drowning you, or perhaps destroying water mills and even smashing dams to flood entire villages!

Don't go swimming after sunset, on a holy day, or without first making the sign of the cross—otherwise, you'll find yourself in deep doggy doo.

Waiting for an unsuspecting bather or fisherman to step close to the water's edge, the vodník will leap out, pulling his victims down to his underwater home, either to drown and eat them or to force them to become his slave.

Only by having a cockerel handy can you save yourself! The vodníci find these birds even more delicious to chow down on than humans!

CASE STUDY 440/26V

While gambling is illegal in the Slavic countries of Russia and the Ukraine, the small country of Belarus is a gambler's paradise, with more than eight thousand casinos and gambling halls!

The Belarusian Gaming Commission recently sent a Gaming Special Agent to investigate reports of illegal gambling in the forest of Kurapaty. The agent e-mailed his findings to the Commission . . . and was never seen again! Here is the agent's final e-mail, with translations from the Belarusian, where necessary!

To: Director BGC

From: GS Agent Salaad Koleslaw

But good! My investigations are finally bearing a full bottle of *uzvar!* (My little humor, Director—*uzvar* being our great country's national drink! *Budzqce zdarovyja!* <Cheers!>)

Yesterday, I come across large pond thick with the bulrushes. There, sitting astride small log is strange little man of illness with green skin.

He is dressed like vagrant, wearing on him plaid shirt, bell-bottom trousers, and straw hat with ribbons. He is looking most mirthful!

"Dobraj ranicy!" <"Good morning!"> I call out in much friendliness of manner, sitting down on large rock. I ask, *"Jak vas zavucq?"* <"What's your name?"> Comes the reply, "Vodník!" I introduce my own to him and inquire of where he lives. He is pointing to water and saying, "Vodník!"

Much puzzled, I try once more in communications. *"Dze vy pracuece?"* <"What do you do for a living?"> I am requiring to know. Into pocket he reaches and pulls out full deck of playing cards. "Vodník!"

Aha! Am then realizing that this is suspected person of illegal gambling! Much excited, I watch little man leap off log and come join me on rock.

He begins upon dealing out of the cards. Much quickly, I am understanding that he wants to play the poker!

To be gaining the truest evidence, I must act the foolishness, so explain that I am not good at the cards. The little man smiles like wolf and replies, "Vodník!"

We are playing all the afternoon, and he is trying the naughty cheat, but is now the one with foolishness because as you are of knowing, Director, I am the expert gambling! Soon I am winning all the games!

At first, little man's eyes blaze like red-hot coals with the anger! Then he smiles and dives into water, reappearing with lidded porcelain cup. Aha! I am of the realizing. He wants to show off to me his collection of crockery!

"Ranicaj!" <"In the morning!"> I am telling him, making off with departing. "I shall be the coming back for you on the morrow!" Little man is unknowing, Director, that I shall be of returning to arrest him for illegal gambling!

"Vodník!" he mirthfully chuckles, holding up cup to wish me good leaving. "Vodník!"

If only little man knew, eh, Director?!

S. Koleslaw

HOW TO GET RID OF A VODNÍK

Fill a super-strong rubber chicken with massive amounts of helium and tether it in the forest, beside a pond or river. When the vodník attacks the bird, release the rope. The vodník will go flying straight up into the stratosphere!

VODNÍK FACT FILE

Location: Slavic countries
Appearance: Green, blue, or gray old dude with long, scraggly beard and covered in slimy gunk
Strength: Strong enough to pull an adult human underwater!
Weaknesses: Seawater—it kills them!
Powers: Shape-shifters. Soul-stealers.
Fear Factor: 34.6

And last but not least on our worldwide tour to track down the most deadly of fae and elementals, we come to the no-holds-barred kookiest creature that ever set foot in the pages of our *Monster Hunters Unlimited* series (well, until we come across an even crazier one!).

May we proudly introduce the mondo-bizarro, messed-up wood elemental better known as—the Whintosser!

This mean-spirited, bad-tempered, troublemaking creep first appeared around the Coast Ranges of California in 1906, having hitchhiked from Central America.

(Geography note: Central America is the central portion of the Americas—duh, obviously!—and is made up of seven countries: Belize, Costa Rica, El Salvador, Guatemala, Honduras, Nicaragua, and Panama.)

You want weird? This bristly, fur-covered beastie's appearance is bugged-out freakish!

Small of size, his head and short tail are attached to the body by a swivel, which allows them to rotate at one hundred revolutions per minute!

Even grosser: Its body is elongated and *Toblerone*-shaped, and it possesses *three* extra pairs of legs! The legs are set at all angles around the body, enabling it to walk upright, sideways, on its back, and even upside down!

First documented in the 1910 field guide *Fearsome Creatures of the Lumberwoods, With A Few Desert and Mountain Beasts* by Minnesota's first State Forrester and Commissioner of Conservation, William Thomas Cox (1878–1961), the Whintosser's infamy spread like wildfire!

Hard-drinking lumberjacks soon found themselves running afoul of this demonic elemental in woodlands across America.

Due to its screwy shape, the Whintosser is a bugbear to kill. As Cox notes in his book, the Whintosser may be "*shot, clubbed, or strung on a pike pole without stopping the wriggling, whirling motions or the screams of rage.*"

CASE STUDY 398/66W

In previous centuries, burly lumberjacks enjoyed sitting around the forest campfire at night, telling scary stories to while away those long, lonely hours. Many of these stories were based on true events.

Here is one we discovered recently, dating back to the early twentieth century!

NEVER MAKE PROMISES WITH THE DEVIL

Not so very long ago as is judged today, Guillermo Jerez, a migratory worker from Guatemala, arrived in the verdant redwood forests of Sierra, California, and found work at a small logging camp.

Sent to join a logging crew, Jerez was put to work helping to fell trees, some more than three hundred feet in height!

"¡Madre Mía!" Jerez groaned that evening, staggering inside the cold, dark shanty he shared with the other lumberjacks, his muscles screaming in agony.

He collapsed exhaustedly onto his bunk bed. "We are paid by the number of trees we cut down, and I managed but two today."

Jerez could hear the other men whispering irritably in the gloom of the log house, which was lit by the dim light of a kerosene lamp.

They were complaining about Jerez and how slow he was. This made Jerez extremely angry.

"I will show them," Jerez hissed when the men eventually fell asleep. "I will cut down more trees than they do tomorrow, and every day!"

That night, Jerez made a pact with the Devil himself!

If the Devil would help Jerez cut down more trees than the other lumberjacks, then Jerez would never again say mass or utter the name of God.

"If you break this promise," said the Devil, bemused, "I shall have your soul."

The next day, when the men started work, Jerez went off alone.

In a small clearing, he found a strange beast waiting for him.

Jerez knew that the creature, which was long and triangular of shape, with a spinning head and tail and five sets of legs, was there to make sure he kept his word to the Devil.

"Do not worry, minion of Satan," snorted Jerez contemptuously, swinging his ax. "If the Devil keeps his word, I shall keep mine."

The blade struck a tree but once——THUUD!——and the tree toppled over, crashing to the ground!

Jerez was astonished! "Unbelievable! ...impossible!" he laughed delightedly.

The creature merely smiled, biding its time.

Again and again, the ax of Jerez struck home. And the trees fell like apple blossoms.

When Jerez rested an hour later, hundreds of trees lay on the ground. He could contain his excitement no longer.

"¡Dios Mío!" he cried out. "I am going to be rich! Rich!"

The creature's eyes blazed like red-hot coals. Howling savagely, it sprang at the terrified Guillermo Jerez!

The Guatemalan's harrowing death screams echoed throughout the forest!

"¡Aiiiiiiiiiiiiiiiiiiiiiiiiii!"

Dropping their tools, the startled lumberjacks rushed to the clearing.

There, they found Jerez's shredded and bloodied clothes, a pile of bones, and a human skull, all picked clean.

"¡Dios Mío!" gasped a fearful Spaniard. "My God!"

THE END

Spanish translations:

Madre mía!: My mother! (Goodness me!)

Guau!: Wow!

Esto es increíble: That is amazing

Dios Mío!: My God!

WHINTOSSER FACT FILE

Location: Central and North America
Appearance: Long, triangular body with three sets of legs, spinning head and tail—basically, bonkers!
Strength: Powerful
Weaknesses: Trick it into a drainage pipe. All of its feet will touch the sides at once and it will walk off in different directions, tearing its body apart!
Powers: Neat spinning head and tail trick
Fear Factor: 62

WHAT TO DO WITH A CAPTURED WHINTOSSER

BLEMMYES

Location: North and West Africa
Appearance: Acephalous (headless) giants whose eyes and mouth are situated in their chest. Freaky!
Strength: Prodigious
Weaknesses: Fresh flesh; they can't get enough of it! Anthropophagi (Greek for man-eaters. The ancient Geek historian Herodotus—who lived circa 484–425 BC—first coined the phrase in his sweeping saga *Histories*, written in the mid fifth century BC). The cannibalistic Blemmyes eat anything on two legs, including themselves!
Powers: None
Fear Factor: 91.6

BUGGANE

Location: Underground, in forests, ancient ruins, or waterfalls on the Isle of Man, a small island between Great Britain and Ireland
Appearance: Ogre status. A mane of thick, coarse black hair; black, wrinkled skin; fiery red eyes; a large red mouth; shining tusks; razor-sharp claws; and hooves. May also disguise itself as a horse, cow, or even as a human—although in human form, it will have long hair, teeth, and nails.
Strength: It enjoys ripping off church roofs, so kind of tough!
Weaknesses: Sunlight. Cannot cross water or enter hallowed ground (ground that has been blessed by a priest, shaman, druid, etc.).
Powers: Shape-shifter
Fear Factor: 44.4

DRAC

Location: The Rhône River in the town of Beaucaire, France
Appearance: Dragon with long snout; blue-green scales; horns; huge, snakelike tail; and ginormous wings. Can take human form, both male and female.
Strength: Immensely strong
Weaknesses: If you discover one, let us know!
Powers: Invisibility. Shape-shifter. Flight. Will hold a glittering object just under the surface of the river to entice bathing young men and women to catch it. The Drac then pulls them down to the depths. Sometimes the victims are eaten; others, especially women, are kept alive to nurse Drac young, and returned to the surface unharmed after seven years.
Fear Factor: 87

DUENDE

Location: Forests, caves, vineyards, and abandoned houses in the Iberian Peninsula (Spain, Portugal, France, Andorra, and Gibraltar), Latin America, the Philippines, and the Mariana Islands in the Pacific Ocean
Appearance: Short, ugly faerie or goblin, approximately one to four feet in height; long, sticking-out ears; full beard; long arms and teeth; black, brown, gray, blond, or red hair; yellowish-brown wrinkly skin. A hole in the left hand. Their feet have pointed heels and are sometimes reversed. Usually decked out in big cone hats, red or green clothes, or animal skins.
Strength: These guys are pip-squeaks
Weaknesses: The color red. Math problems (they're useless with any number past twelve). Milk and chocolate (they love the stuff!). A baby's dirty diaper. (We don't blame them! Pooo-ooo!)
Powers: Invisibility. Shape-shifting. Hypnotic whistling (used to lure young women into the forest, causing them to become lost, and to persuade mothers to give up their child for the duende to eat!). Soul-stealers. One look can turn you to stone.
Fear Factor: 50

GREMLINS

Location: United Kingdom, United States, Germany

Appearance: Either tiny humans with large, pointy ears and yellow eyes wearing overalls, or short, hideous creatures with large bat ears and glowing red or green eyes

Strength: Lack physical power, so work together to achieve their aims

Weaknesses: A gremlin bell made from bronze or brass, which will ward off their magic and make them violently sick. Cold (magical) iron. Predatory animals, such as cats and eagles.

Powers: Magic. Concealment. Also, the ability to crash computers, destroy important documents, feed homework to the dog, mess with the hot and cold water in showers, cause humans to bang their thumb with a hammer, puncture tires, stop clocks, burst water pipes. In fact, if anything goes wrong, it's probably the fault of a gremlin. Able to sabotage all types of machinery, and especially enjoy messing with airplanes.

Fear Factor: If you're thirty thousand feet in the air and a gremlin strikes, we're guessing 1,000,000! Otherwise between 20–80, give or take.

IKAKI

Location: Nigeria, West Africa

Appearance: A very small, mischievous, and cantankerous water spirit that has the shape of a tortoise

Strength: Tortoise-y

Weaknesses: Magic spells

Powers: The Dance—of Death! We kid you not! When Ikaki starts doing the samba, humans drop dead! And then it eats you! Although, being a tortoise, no guess that it almost ... ga ... in ... g

Fear Factor: 8 (Uh, go on there,) but probably because we're feeling generous.)

OVINNIK

Location: The corners of threshing houses (barns) in Slavic countries, notably Russia and the Ukraine
Appearance: A large black cat with ruffled fur that barks like a dog
Strength: Not impressive
Weaknesses: Loud noises, especially thunder or fireworks
Powers: Can predict the future. If angered or neglected, will set fire to the grain stored in the threshing house, with the owners trapped inside.
Fear Factor: 19.1

POOKA

Location: Mountains and hills of the United Kingdom, Ireland, the Channel Islands (Jersey and Guernsey in the English Channel), France, Germany, Scandinavia, Norway, United States
Appearance: The "oldest old thing in England," the Pooka is thousands of years old. A shape-shifter, it takes on whichever form it fancies. It can look like a deformed goblin, a hairy Bogeyman, a frightening creature with the head of a donkey, a demon with wings, a silver-haired elf, an eagle with ginormous wings, a goat with curled horns, a horse, a rabbit, a dog, or a sleek black horse with sulphurous yellow eyes and long, wild mane. Whatever its shape, its hair or fur is always jet-black.
Strength: Magical
Weaknesses: Cold iron

Powers: Shape-shifting. Invisibility. Flight (will swoop down on night travelers and throw them into muddy ditches). Magic. Powerful curses (can stop hens from laying eggs and cows from producing milk). A vindictive vandal, the Pooka enjoys tearing down gates and fences and destroying crops. Can spread infectious disease and cause illness in livestock.
Fear Factor: 41

RAROG

Location: Poland
Appearance: Dwarf, raven, or killer whirlwind
Strength: Tremendous
Weaknesses: Throw a knife into the center of the whirlwind to pierce the heart and kill the Rarog inside. Or shout the magic spell, "My belt around your neck!" to strangle it. (Of course, the Rarog whirlwind will probably suck out all of your breath before you have a chance to incant, so the best of luck with that one!)
Powers: Shape-shifter. Flight
Fear Factor: 78

SASABONSAM

Location: Togo, Ghana, and the Ivory Coast, West Africa
Appearance: Hairy, thin ogre with red skin, bloodshot eyes, stubby arms, iron teeth, long legs with iron hooks for feet—the feet pointing both ways—and hooked wings spanning twenty feet.
Strength: There aren't many weakling ogres that we know about, so we're reckoning on immensely powerful!
Weaknesses: Magic spells might work, and possibly the old stake-through the heart trick . . . if you can get that close!
Powers: A bloodsucking vampire who sits on the high branches of a tree to catch travelers between its legs before it devours them. (Tip: Look for a dark red color on the bare ground beneath a tree. Chances are it's the spilled blood of the Sasabonsam's victims!)
Fear Factor: 96.3

SPRIGGANS

Location: Barrows and castle ruins, Cornwall, UK

Appearance: Small, grotesquely ugly wizened old man with a child's head, crooked features and body, spindly limbs, and oversized feet. They wear pieces of stone on their clothes. (They are considered ghosts of or descendants of giants.)

Strength: Strong

Weaknesses: Wearing your clothes inside out. Cold iron. Holy water.

Powers: One of the most wicked of the fae. Act as faerie bodyguards and guard buried treasure. Consummate thieves. Shape-shifters; they can grow to enormous size when threatened. Control the weather, creating howling storms and whirlwinds. Can spread illnesses, blight crops, destroy buildings, lead travelers into mortal danger, and steal babies from cradles, leaving changelings in their place. Prone to violence.

Fear Factor: 89

VIBRIA

Location: Caves and underground lairs of the Catalan communities of Spain, France, and Italy (including the areas of Catalonia, Valencia, the Balearic Islands—Majorca, Ibiza, and Minorca—Andorra, and the Italian city of Alghero)

Appearance: Female dragon with an eagle's beak instead of a dragon's snout. Only possesses clawed hind legs and has a huge wingspan.

Strength: It's a dragon!! (You know, not a wimp!)

Weaknesses: If you survive the encounter with a vibria, we'd love to know how you did it!

Powers: Immortal. Flight. Magical blood. Breathes fire and poisonous breath.

Fear Factor: 81.5